# Bello:
# hidden talent rediscovered

Bello is a digital only imprint of Pan Macmillan,
established to breathe new life into previously published,
classic books.

At Bello we believe in the timeless power of the imagination,
of good story, narrative and entertainment and we want to use
digital technology to ensure that many more readers
can enjoy these books into the future.

We publish in ebook and Print on Demand formats
to bring these wonderful books to new audiences.

*About Bello:*

www.panmacmillan.com/bello

*Sign up to our newsletter to hear about*
*new releases, events and competitions:*

www.panmacmillan.com/bellonews

*Jo Bannister*

Jo Bannister lives in Northern Ireland, where she worked as a journalist and editor on local newspapers. Since giving up the day job, her books have been shortlisted for a number of awards. Most of her spare time is spent with her horse and dog, or clambering over archaeological sites. She is currently working on a new series of psychological crime/thrillers.

*Jo Bannister*

# THE WINTER
# PLAIN

BELL

First published in 1982 by Hale

This edition published 2012 by Bello
an imprint of Pan Macmillan, a division of Macmillan Publishers Limited
Pan Macmillan, 20 New Wharf Road, London N1 9RR
Basingstoke and Oxford
Associated companies throughout the world

www.panmacmillan.com/imprints/bello

ISBN 978-1-4472-3640-5 EPUB
ISBN 978-1-4472-3639-9 POD

Copyright © Jo Bannister, 1982

The right of Jo Bannister to be identified as the
author of this work has been asserted in accordance
with the Copyright, Designs and Patents Act 1988.

Every effort has been made to contact the copyright holders of the material
reproduced in this book. If any have been inadvertently overlooked, the publisher
will be pleased to make restitution at the earliest opportunity.

You may not copy, store, distribute, transmit, reproduce or otherwise
make available this publication (or any part of it) in any form, or by any means
(electronic, digital, optical, mechanical, photocopying, recording or otherwise),
without the prior written permission of the publisher. Any person who does
any unauthorized act in relation to this publication may be liable to
criminal prosecution and civil claims for damages.

The Macmillan Group has no responsibility for the information provided by
any author websites whose address you obtain from this book ('author websites').
The inclusion of author website addresses in this book does not constitute
an endorsement by or association with us of such sites or the content,
products, advertising or other materials presented on such sites.

This book remains true to the original in every way. Some aspects may appear
out-of-date to modern-day readers. Bello makes no apology for this, as to retrospectively
change any content would be anachronistic and undermine the authenticity of the original.
Bello has no responsibility for the content of the material in this book. The opinions
expressed are those of the author and do not constitute an endorsement by,
or association with, us of the characterization and content.

A CIP catalogue record for this book is available from the British Library.

Printed and bound by CPI Group (UK) Ltd, Croydon, CR0 4YY

Visit **www.panmacmillan.com** to read more about all our books
and to buy them. You will also find features, author interviews and
news of any author events, and you can sign up for e-newsletters
so that you're always first to hear about our new releases.

# Strangers

# Chapter One

The man with three camels arrived in time to witness the execution but too late to take any part in the events leading up to it. He found a stable lofty enough for his animals and left the cow and calf there with his packs, but the bull he took with him when he returned to the square. Camels seldom percolated this far into the Ice Desert, so that the supercilious sand-coloured creature drew stares even on that frenzied day. Paul used them because they could carry more, faster, over worse terrain than a horse and could be relied upon to fight dirty in a tight corner.

Chad was known as the Garden City in the golden days before the war. A stable monarchy and a democratic council had created between them a city state of such vitality that its people had conquered the desert for miles around, making it blossom with farms and flowers. The hot mineral spring which was the fount of such bounty provided warm homes in the middle of the tundra, irrigation warm enough to penetrate the permafrost, and a perennial source of several chemicals invaluable to an isolated industrialised city.

The mineral spring – an unimpressive thing it was, too, when you went into the well house and looked at it bubbling turgidly from the stained rocks – was the beginning of Chad, the reason the Garden City had survived and thrived when other settlements froze to death in the desert, but real sophistication came to the Chad culture with the development of an energy source to pump the water great distances, purify it, process its minerals and confer other benefits unassociated with the spring. Chad had nuclear power. The man with the camels was a nuclear engineer.

It was two years since Paul was last in the Garden City. Then the war with Harry Jess, earl of the Northlands, was only a distant gathering cloud, a vague anxiety. The king had said, off-handedly, that nothing but wind ever came out of the north, and had professed to take more interest in valves and control rods than the threat to his small, prosperous kingdom. Paul had wondered at the time if the king, who was no mere figurehead, neither witless nor naive, were genuinely unaware of the danger or found it politic to feign unconcern.

And now, two years later, the Barbarian was in Chad. His hordes had turned its gracious, leisurely streets into a running melee. Broken things littered the pavements. Dead bodies piled up in places where the invaders thought it humourous: the courthouse was one, the library another. Most of them dated back a week to the first sacking of the city.

Now the king who had professed indifference towards the menace from the north, having already lost his realm, was about to yield up his life. Nothing Paul knew about Harry Jess suggested he would make it easy.

Holding the bull by a short leash and using the unease provoked by its great loose-limbed body to open a channel for him through the pressing crowd, he made for the centre of the immense square. As long as Chad had stood this square had been its heart, and for the last hundred years the heart of the square had been its ornamental fountain. The statue posing in the bronze bowl, of the ruler who had it made, was tall but lacking any other merit, but its moving waters were both a delight to the senses and a testament to the culture which made streams to flow in the immutable tundra. In the Ice Desert living water was the hallmark of man.

The tall statue was toppled and sprawled in a shattered line across the cobbles. Some of the smaller pieces had already been pilfered, as souveniers or to be hammered or cast into swords and speartips and arrowheads by Barbarian warriors. A greater loss was the sound of the fountain, silenced by the crudely effective means of an axe-blow to the supply pipe. The precious water ran to waste across the cobbles and wet the watchers' feet.

The destruction of the fountain was not wanton, as it might well have been, but a means of adapting the bronze bowl to an end it could not have served full of water. The cauldron was heaped with coals, and amid them the ragged figure of the king was bound to the surviving lower left leg of his deposed ancestor. The tableau left absolutely no room for doubt as to how it would unfold.

The man with the camel knew the king at once, which was perhaps surprising in view of the state of him; but then the whole ambience of the square prepared Paul for what he must see. Also, the king had come through the monstrous trials of the last days into the calm no-mans-land before death, stripped of hope but also of despair; confident that the peace he was about to gain was more desirable than the life he would lose, King John II of the City State of Chad was more recognisably himself than at any time since the Barbarian's torturers got their hands on him.

From his vantage above the sea of heads John looked his last upon his Garden City, seeing its marred beauty as a reflection of his own and not sorry to be leaving before injury turned to corruption and defeat to degradation. His mind, skimming mosquito-like across the surface of awareness, touched briefly on the Chad of his childhood, his father and brothers; upon his own reign, the advances he had made, the mistakes; upon the ill-fated campaign to resist incursion from the Northlands. The last days had been painful for him not only because of what they had done to him but also because of the rape of Chad. Many, many times he had ridden through this square and seen friends faces, rosy with prosperity. Now he recognised no one, saw only fear on the faces of his people, driven here by the gloating horde, the exits from the square blocked by champing horses and grinning Northmen in bright-studded surcoats. They were right to be afraid: most of them would follow him sooner rather than later, and he had no wish to share their extra weeks of life at the cost of grief and slavery. His death would be quicker than theirs, so perhaps less cruel.

The one thing the king did not think of, as his gaze skated distantly over the scene, was his son. He had spent too many days keeping that thought out of his mind, lest in agony he should betray it, to admit it now. Yet, as someone dropped a torch among the coals with less ceremony than might have been expected, something caught his fading eye to provoke the forbidden thought. It was not Edmund, but it was a young man, someone he knew, someone he once knew watching him through the mounting flames with neither horror nor delight but a kind of cold, clear assurance that made no sense until he realised that the great gravel-coloured bulk beside him was not the figment of a fever-dream.

When his eyes and the king's met across the leaping, climbing flames Paul recognised several facts simultaneously: that the king knew him; that he suspected, at however instinctive a level, the reason for his presence; that he had arrived too late to earn the inertial navigation system even if the quadro-dimensional navigator was still within his reach; and that burning to death was a slow and not very merciful way to go.

The packed square erupted in chaos as the big bull camel bucked and bellowed and spun round, clearing a space for itself by the simple expedient of trampling some people under its spreading pneumatic feet and projecting others, screaming, into still closer contact with their neighbours with a swing of its great woolly quarters. In the free-for-all which followed, with civilians trying to fight their way clear of the rabid beast and soldiers trying to fight their way towards it, almost none of the thousands present saw that the king was dead before the flames hid him from view, his eye pierced through by a slender dart.

Of the few who did, one was a girl attending on Harry Jess as he watched the execution from a second-storey balcony of the royal palace. What distinguished Sharvarim-besh from all the others, including the earl of the Northlands, was the mere accident of her birth: raised far south of Chad, in a caravanserai town athwart the trading routes, she was familiar with the sight of camels and was not distracted by the antics of this one from the historic events being enacted below. So she saw the king die minutes before the crowd believed it witnessed his death.

Sheer surprise made her startle and gasp, and she might have spoken had anyone at all showed signs of having seen the same thing. But not a murmur rose from the mob, while Harry Jess was bent forward over the parapet, enjoying the spectacle of the beast as a comic interlude before the main entertainment which would begin when the fire, unheralded by anaesthetic smoke, reached his vanquished adversary. Shah actually had her hand on his arm to tell him what she had seen, but he shook her off and on reflection she decided she had seen nothing. She had not wanted to see the king burn, and she had no wish to bring down the earl's vengeance on whoever had taken advantage of the sudden chaos to perform that last service for his sovereign. Travelling with Harry she had seen decimation before: she had no wish to precipitate a fresh massacre here. So she leaned over the balcony with the Barbarian earl, and looked where he pointed and laughed when he laughed, and when he claimed to hear the king's screams above the cheers of his soldiers and the crump of flames she gave no indication that she knew he was deluding himself.

Later, after the crowd had dispersed, the shocked hush broken only by a few hysterical voices as the satisfied soldiery drove appalled citizens back to their sacked homes, Shah was still with the earl when the new palace guard brought the man with the camel to him.

He came surrounded by blades and touched by none of them. His bearing, as he walked the length of the room, was self-assured.

The sergeant of the guard said. "He injured Ap-Rel."

He sounded sullen and wary.

"Is that the cretin with the spear? I told him to keep it out of my back but he wouldn't listen. I think I broke his neck. I certainly intended to."

Harry Jess had enjoyed his day and was in a tolerant frame of mind; also he felt that the spectacle with the camel was worth the loss of one soldier, particularly Ap-Rel. He was just mellow enough to be intrigued rather than incensed at arrogance on the part of a camel-drover. Arms akimbo, his sparse frame angled forward in a stance more usually assumed by bigger men, with a good humour rather chilling in view of the words themselves, he inquired. "Have you been so long in the Ice Desert that you don't know who I am, how many people I have killed to get here, how many I shall kill to stay here, and how much it might amuse me to make you one of them?"

Shah's great eyes blinked wide at the sudden wolfish grin which split the man's wind-darkened face. His face was as knowingly enigmatic as a temple maks, its deeply graven lines satiric, its gold-flecked obsidian eyes sardonically watchful. It was a cruel face, she thought, as cruel in its subtler way as the earl's. Physically too he was like Harry, an inch shorter but the same spare frame, wiry rather than muscular. He used his body as a cat does, with awareness and deliberation and with that feline aura of latent savagery. But his mind came as a complete shock. It was nothing like Harry's, incomparably greater: a sprawling intellect, its boundaries pushed out far beyond her ability to map them, its inner regions dense and complex and so active that she withdrew with a gasp, drawing a sharp glance from Harry and the quirk of a lip from the temple mask. His face gave absolutely no warning of the machine inside his head. The only real thing he and Harry had in common was the anger.

"Yes, I know you, Harry Jess." Scorn radiated from him. "You haven't changed much. You used to be a bully, now you're a tyrant. That's a change of scale, not of degree. You've not got bigger: only fatter."

Shah stopped breathing. So did the earl, to the point that he started going blue. Then he whispered with conviction. "I shall have you flayed and your skin hung from the ramparts."

Paul laughed. "You're not even original. You'll do nothing, because you're a coward and if there's one way you can be sure of bringing every war-machine in the Ice Desert down on your stupid head it's by harming me. While nuclear power is all that makes the northern cities viable, I'm the safest man on the tundra."

"You'd better be," hissed Jess. "Who are you?"

"I'm an engineer. I am in fact, so far as Chad and the other cities of the Ice Desert are concerned, *the* engineer. I came here to service the king's pile. It doesn't matter to me that it's now your pile, so long as you can pay for the job, but I'd better warn you that without servicing it'll slump down in about three months' time."

"What does that mean?"

Paul frowned, looked round for somewhere to sit and dropped into a chair without waiting for an invitation. "You don't know much about what you've stolen, do you? Look. The valves on the cooling system have a safe working life of 27 months. They're now two years old. When they fail the coolant stops flowing. The pile generates enough heat to melt the bottom of the callandria containing it and slumps down into the foundations of the city. Chad will lose power, gain irradiation and quite possibly disappear into a morass of suddenly liquid permafrost. That's three ways to lose your new kingdom, Harry Jess."

"I remember," Harry said slowly. "I remember where we met. Your name is Paul."

"I thought I was going to have to tell you that too."

"And hers was Elaine."

Paul grinned at Shah. "Never mind, you got a new one."

Reaching out hesitantly, Shah found in Harry's head the familiar, frightening passion. His temper was a devil which rode him and fed him; at its height it had the explosive vigour of an epilepsy. Colder than that was this clear-headed fury, more terrible in its reasoning hatred than all his mindless raging. He said carefully, "I think it will be worth Chad to me to watch you die. A man can do a lot of dying in three months." Shah could almost taste the savour of anticipation on his lips.

"It'll cost you more than Chad, Harry. The only barter you can buy my life with is your own. I'm a busy man: I'm due in Leshkas inside the month. Their state, like Chad, depends on an obsolete, overworked, inexpertly run nuclear power plant which is overdue a service. If I don't get there on time, they're going to want to know why. When they find that by killing the only nuclear engineer north of the tree line you have condemned their entire culture, they're going to come after you with a flame-thrower. Nor will they be alone: the other ten cities which will sooner or later perish without me will also wish to mark their disapproval in some positive fashion."

That he had his faults was undeniable, but the Earl of the Northlands was not stupid. In the decade since inheriting his domain on the never wholly explained demise of his uncle, Harry Jess had welded an impoverished feudal province into a fortress and a disordered population into an effective fighting force. He had trained them, armed them, made them mobile with horses, and set forth conquering and to conquer. Now he was rich, powerful, feared far beyond the Northlands; but he was not so powerful as to confound an assault by the combined forces of the desert cities, and neither his wealth nor his reputation would save him from doomed men avenging their own destruction. His fury was not such as to blind him to the engineer's peculiar invulnerability, nor to persuade him that the satisfaction of killing him would be worth the risk involved. Being rich, powerful and feared gave a man a lot to lose.

So, at least for the moment, Harry Jess owned himself out-manoeuvred and shrugged. "After all, she was only a slave."

"Not any more."

"You didn't keep her?"

"She's now a high priestess at Oracle. She prays for my soul."

"That must be comforting."

"Not as much as the people counting off the days in Leshkas."

"And then," Shah told the poet, "he turned his back and walked out. Harry was livid. He snatched a spear off the sergeant of the guard and hefted it over his shoulder. I really thought he was going to throw it. I tried to warn the engineer – I told you, I thought maybe he was a telepath – but he just kept going and Harry seemed to realise what he was doing and hurled the spear into the panelling beside the door instead. The man just grinned at it as he went through. Afterwards Harry did this." She indicated her eye.

"One day," prophesied Itzhak, applying salve and powder with deft fingers, "he'll go too far and scar you, and then he won't want you around any more."

"You think I don't know that? But what can I do?"

"The first thing you'd better do is make sure he never finds out you're rooting for the opposition."

"He'll never know that," averred Shah. "He doesn't know I'm telepathic, and he's not going to. No one here does, except you."

"I know," he replied wistfully. "You wanted to confide in someone and I was the most harmless, inconsequential clown you could find."

Her hand closed over his. "You have been my refuge. Your friendship has kept me sane. It's the most valuable gift anyone has ever given me."

The poet's sad, sweet smile lit the grey room. "I live for you," he said simply. "But Shah, for your own safety, remember that I am a coward and, much as I might wish it otherwise, I cannot die for you. If Harry Jess ever comes to suspect you and quizzes me, I will tell him. I shall hate myself and wish myself unborn, but if I can save myself by betraying you I shall not hesitate to do it."

"I know," she said kindly, patting his hand. "Don't worry about it. It will never happen."

# Chapter Two

Paul first saw the crooked man in the square and thought nothing of it. Most of Chad, and most of the Northlanders too, were there then. Later he had seen him in the palace, scurrying along the corridor close to the wall like the other menials. But now here he was again, humping hay in the stables, hefting and hurling the bales mechanically, one eye on the door. Paul slipped back unseen and stood thoughtfully a moment, questing his memory, while his agile craftsman's fingers strayed unconsciously to his belt, checking the weapons there, keeping them loose and ready. When he stepped through the door he knew both who the man was and what he wanted.

Paul made very few mistakes. It was a question not of pride but of survival. Men of his profession – of both his professions – fell into but two categories: the careful and the dead. Nevertheless, he made one of those rare mistakes when he walked past the labouring man and, offering it fruit from his pocket, remarked to the camel, "So Chad still has a king."

Instinct rather than sight or hearing registered the movement behind him, the unexpected velocity, and he was already turning when a swinging fist like a morning-star crashed against his temple, exploding lights in his eyes and sending him reeling in the straw. Two thoughts raced through his head – that, unlikely as it was coming from an old cripple, he should have anticipated the assault, and that he was probably now fighting for his life – and were as swiftly gone as his mind moved into that overdrive condition in which mental and physical powers achieve communion. His hand was at his waist before he could see again, but the crooked man had gone with him as he rolled and kicked his wrist away: pain shot up to his shoulder-blade. Ignoring it, Paul rolled over the arm and got his feet under him. As he rose the cripple swung again: his boot connected forcefully with Paul's jaw, crashing him backwards into the stable partition behind, his head colliding dully with the inch-thick wood. Under the combined effects of three concussive blows inside ten seconds Paul's senses deserted him and, unconscious, his body crumpled and slumped along the timber wall.

Lockwood slapped him awake, but not before taking the precaution of wiring his hands behind him and his neck to the wooden upright carrying the stable door. Surprise had won him the encounter – nobody ever expected a hunchback to fight – but that advantage was now lost and Lockwood suspected, with the shrewd judgement of a man to whom such assessments were a matter of professional competence, that when he started feeling more like his old self this one could give trouble. Being a professional, Lockwood had no silly scruples about fair play: he tied the man up and then started hitting him.

Paul was not far away and when he came round he came fast, so fast he had started to move before he realised that the situation had changed. He was brought up short by the wire noose biting into his throat. The crooked man thumped him back against the stall and kept him there with one spread hand on his chest. The hand was enormous. Belatedly Paul recognised that the whole man was enormous, with long powerful arms, muscular from a lifetime's industry, and short strong thighs. Even the distorted back had bent into an arch of strength, like a bow or a bridge. Crooked he was. Cripple he was not.

After he had surprised people with the effectiveness of his twisted body, Lockwood usually surprised them afresh with his voice. There is no law, either natural or of men, that hunchbacks come exclusively from the lower classes, but that particular blend of education and authority, the mellow tone with the steely edge that comes of being obeyed, tended to knock the breath out of people who had just got used to the shape of him.

A blade flickered dimly in his hand. He said, "I don't know who you are or what you're doing here, and the only reason you're alive now is so that you can tell me. One usually allows a little time for bluster, but if you know that you're too dangerous to have around that long. So the first lie you tell me will cost you your left eye. The second will cost you your right eye, and if you're still capable of lying after that I shall tighten this thing until it cuts your throat." He demonstrated briefly. "Now, do we understand each other?"

When he could breath again Paul, his flecked eyes flashing with fury, choked, "You damn fool, Lockwood, if I meant to harm the boy I'd be talking to Harry Jess, not you."

Lockwood nodded. "I thought of that. Then I thought perhaps you already had." His knife had found a resting place on Paul's bloody cheek, its chill point just puckering the outer corner of his eye. "That seemed a reasonable explanation of why you were taken into the palace by guards but left alone."

"It wouldn't explain how you left, though, would it?"

Lockwood was watching him very carefully. Beaten, bound, possibly not an enemy anyway, he still struck the hunchback as a formidable opponent. "Perhaps they hoped I would lead them to him."

"That would be naive. Also unnecessary. I know where he is."

In all his dangerous days Paul had probably never been closer to death than at that moment. A shutter seemed to fall behind Lockwood's eyes. He took a handful of Paul's hair and bent his head back, baring his throat for the execution stroke. He actually muttered the formal exculpation, then with the knife already poised, paused. "By all of heaven – *how* did you know?"

"You told me," Paul managed. The effort of speaking seemed to tear his jugular.

Lockwood's eyes, which had cleared fractionally, blanked over again. "I warned you about lying." Searching the young man's face he saw the obsidian eyes flick sideways and suddenly remembered what was behind him. He said swiftly, "One word to that beast and whatever it does as a result you won't live to see it."

"Then Emir will kill you and there will be no one left to rescue the boy."

The logic was inescapable. Slowly Lockwood dropped his knife-hand, released his hold on his captive. "Explain."

"You," sneered Paul. "You betray him just by being here. Once I realised who you were – and let's face it, there aren't that many people answering your description – it followed that the prince was still here. If both the king and his son were dead, there was no way both you and Harry Jess would be alive. But I've seen Harry and I saw the king die. The only thing keeping you from a suicide raid on his murderer is your duty to his son. If you'd been able to get him out by now you wouldn't be here: it's too soon for you to have taken him to safety and returned, and anyway you wouldn't be so afraid of discovery. I've seen you in the palace, coming and going as if you'd every right to be there. You've known that rambling old pile for fifty years: what better place to hide a prince than the rabbit-warrens of his own palace? But for some reason he's less able to move around than you – because if you, who are fairly recognisable, can get in and out one 16-year-old boy in a city with hundreds of them should have no difficulty; and yet he's still here. Is he sick, hurt, what?"

Lockwood stared at him until his eyes started to dry up and then he blinked. Then he said flatly, "Nobody thinks that good."

Paul grinned, the feral gleam splitting his bruised and bloody face. "I do."

"Are you a magician?" Lockwood was an educated, intelligent and experienced man, a professional soldier, and he was absolutely serious.

"That's right. I'm the magician who conjures the mysterious power machine in your backyard."

"The pile?" Lockwood frowned, not understanding; then slowly recognition dawned. "Wait a minute, I know you – you've been here before —"

"Several times. If you wish to pursue this conversation, might I suggest that you remove the garrotte? – I find it inhibiting."

Lockwood weighed up the risk and decided it was justified. As his powerful fingers worked at the noose he said, "It must be a couple of years ago you were here last. The king told me about you. He said he asked you to stay. He said you refused."

"I like travelling. Cities make me cough."

"And now, precisely now, you're here again. Why did you come?"

"To service the power plant."

"And?"

"To save the king."

A spasm ran through Lockwood's crouching frame, a twitch momentarily catching up one side of his face. "You left it too late."

"I didn't expect Chad to fall so quickly."

Lockwood had directed the ill-starred defence. He swallowed the implicit insult and, breaking the wire binding Paul's hands, rocked back on his heels. "And?"

"To get the boy to safety. I assume that's what you want too."

"Can you do it?"

"Yes."

"*Why* are you doing it?"

Paul rubbed at the wire marks on his wrists, the right more gently than the left. "Someone is paying me."

"In God's name, who?"

"Nobody you know. Someone who will very shortly owe me an ion-drive battle-cruiser."

Edmund dreamed. His dreams were not the usual loosely linked hotch-potch of memories, imaginings and sex. Once he had such dreams and enjoyed them and woken from them refreshed. Now his dreams were brittle, angry, kaleidoscopic progressions of raging images that made no Sense and when he woke, sweating and far-eyed, reality made no sense either. Because incomprehensible dreams are more acceptable than an incomprehensible reality he came to welcome the return of the mind-jangling, strength-sapping sleep, dismissing the increasingly short periods of comparative lucidity as an irrelevance.

Sometimes the perplexing actuality involved a strangely distorted figure crouching over him. Once he woke and saw two figures. He was not sure if there were really two or if it were the strangeness of his perception spreading. As a philosophical problem it seemed to him interesting but incapable of solution and therefore not worth worrying about. Dimly aware that one of the two – if they were two – was slapping his face, and considering it an impertinence, he waited for the brilliant lunacy that would deliver him from assault and from thought. As it came, sweeping through his synapses like a glittering tide, he heard the other – if there were two – say thinly, "God!" Then the madness took him.

"That," Paul said at last, the words falling like drops of acid into the painful silence, "is the rightful king of Chad?" Lockwood nodded miserably. "Are you sure you won't settle for Harry Jess?"

Marginally less depressed the soldier would have reacted with violence. But looking at the ruin of his prince he could only shake his head despondently. "He's not going to have them rallying to him by the thousand, is he?"

"How long has he been like this?"

"He's worse every time I look at him. I don't understand it, he's had nothing for days —"

"What was it – drax?"

"It wasn't his fault, he didn't —"

"Was it drax?" Paul's voice came from the arctic no-man's-land between disinterest and disgust; it was the voice of the tundra itself, chill, uncaring, unforgiving.

"Yes," whispered Lockwood, remembering. He bent suddenly over the boy and tried to cover his lax body with a rag of blanket. "He was wounded at the West Scarp a month ago. That was our first line of defence against the Northlander; it collapsed, of course."

Lockwood remembered the pure, savage beauty of the West Scarp, where the greater of the two glaciers feeding the Ice Desert swept down from the Tantalus Mountains, carving a snowcrusted swathe through towering intransigent rock. The escarpment was a natural barrier protecting the cities of the plain from the barbarian North, but the glacier was a weakness. In Lockwood's youth it had been defended time and again against unorganised marauders, but Harry Jess had built himself an army.

Their studded surcoats had flashed like ice crystals as they came down the glacier, their dark horses snatching impatiently at their bits, pawing with greased hooves and snorting silver breath. They came without haste, their almost casual advance spreading out across the glacier like a broad carpet unrolling down the slope, an inevitability. They maintained this slow progression until their first rank – there were many ranks – came within bow range of the waiting men of Chad; then they struck silver spurs to their horses' flanks and dropped their spearheads to the front, and the thunder of their charge filled the mountain, and the mayhem of their cries rose even above that.

The king was in the centre phalanx of the defence. Edmund, in his first battle, was on the left flank, the flush of excitement on his cheeks, the battle-light like alcohol in his eyes. Lockwood positioned himself close enough to the prince to give support if needed and far enough away to be overlooked if not. He had already given the boy a fighting education, instilled into him the principles of tactics, inculcated in him the priceless instinct for when to ignore them, and drummed into him the lesson of history – that a live king can lead a beaten army back to triumph while a superior force which loses its leader can, with equal contrariness, snatch defeat from the jaws of victory. Lockwood was confident that the prince knew enough and had enough of the right instincts to fight effectively. All he needed now to turn him into a soldier was the tempering fire of real combat; to survive which he would require, in addition to all the skills Lockwood had given him, that which he could not – luck.

The Barbarian also had some notion of tactics. As his foremost charge bore down on the central phalanx the line broke, the galloping arms sweeping smoothly by on either side, scything through the Chad flanks to round on the backs of the defenders as they met the spears of the second rank.

Fortunately the king, who also learned his trade largely from Lockwood, recognised the manoeuvre in time to turn his arrowhead bulwark into a defensive diamond, fenced in by shields and swords. In that formation the pride of the Chad army, invulnerable and unwieldy as a tortoise, staggered under the weight of the attack, tried valiantly but in vain to counter it, then finally acknowledged their position untenable and shuffled off, safely but without dignity, leaving Harry Jess the field.

Both Chad flanks suffered heavy casualties in that first unexpected onslaught. Afterwards those who still stood fought their way through the mêlée of tramping horses and battling men to join their colleagues in the turtle. But the prince was not among them.

Lockwood saw his pupil fall. He saw the encounter shaping up, knew what was about to happen, and was almost close enough to prevent it. After the main body of horsemen had swept through, leaving the margin of the glacier carpeted with casualties, Edmund was still on his feet and rallying his depleted troop about his flashing blade. Lockwood saw blood on his face from a sword scratch but it was plainly superficial and incommoding him not at all.

Then in the tail of the movement came another rider, driving his wild-eyed beast through the thick of the Chad injured in pursuit of his comrades. Lockwood doubted whether the Northerner had marked Edmund as a target before the boy sprang towards him, sword swinging, battle in his eyes and a challenge on his lips. Then the Barbarian, checking his beast's charge momentarily, chucked it sideways towards the prince, couching his spear as he did so.

Even then Edmund could have parried the blow, or avoided it, had he not made the fundamental error common to foot-soldiers on first meeting cavalry: that of assuming the danger to lie in the horse, not the man. He knew better: he had been warned against it, trained against it. But Chad, fighting all its infrequent battles on its own doorstep, had never developed cavalry as an arm of warfare: its few horses were used for transport and for ceremony. Now, in the heat of battle, gut instinct ruling over learnt lessons, Edmund let his attention and his point slide from the spangled warrior to his thundering, innocuous steed. The leather shield which protected his body deflected the spear downwards into his thigh where it lodged, quivering, while the lancer rode away without it, pleased with his marksmanship.

Lockwood reached the shocked youth before he collapsed. With his left arm locked across Edmund's chest and his right wielding a sword no one cared to meet, he cleared a passage through the turmoil and dragged his prince from the field.

"It was a bad wound," Lockwood went on, his voice a dull monotone, "and the pain was bad, and the surgeon gave him drax for the journey back to Chad. After the wound was healing he gave him more so that he could ride through the city with his father to put heart into the people, and after that – well, it kept him going at a time when we needed to appear strong. I should not have permitted it, but we were fighting for survival, I needed every weapon I could get, the prince apparently fit and well was worth a hundred pikes.

"But of course he was neither fit nor well, he was by then verging on breakdown, so before the Barbarians attacked the city I sent him up here with a man to look after him. The city held out for three days; after it fell it was another twenty-four hours before I could come here unseen. I found him much as you see him, and alone; the man had fled. That was five days ago. He's had no drug since but he gets steadily worse. I don't know why. I decided that after he was dead I would go downstairs and try to kill Harry Jess."

Paul said, "His brain's synthesizing the stuff."

Lockwood blinked, returning to the present with an almost physical effort. "What?"

"Painkillers work by matching natural receptors in the brain. The natural match for the receptor, the system's own anaesthetic, is normally very difficult to activate but production of it is stimulated by introduction of the drax which simulates it. That's why a drax junkie can't be dried out – once the habit is established he doesn't even need to fix."

Lockwood, staring into the heartless analytical eyes, felt his own moisten. "It is hopeless, then."

"No. Not necessarily, not if I can get hold of some drax. If I can hook him back onto the synthetic stuff and then wean him slowly off, his own production may not rise again to compensate."

"May not?" echoed Lockwood. "Is that the best you can offer?"

The engineer grinned again. "You still think I'm a magician. The only certainty about this is that if he survives he's going to hurt a whole lot more than a spear in the leg."

"I told you to keep those muscle-bound cretins away from me," snapped Paul, stalking unannounced into the throneroom where Harry Jess was trying on the crown jewels.

"And I told you," the Barbarian said silkily, weighing an orb in his neat hand, "or if I didn't I should have done, to wait for an invitation before coming into my presence."

Paul went over to the window and sat down on the sill, a malicious smile curling his lip. "Keep your threats for the peasants, they might be impressed. And give those baubles to the girl: on you they look ridiculous."

The earl slammed down the orb, denting it, for it was hollow, and kicked the girl away as she proffered a golden torque from the open chest at his feet. Shah retreated a safe distance and sat down on the floor, watching the two men covertly.

"You think you're safe," shouted Harry Jess. "Well, you're not. Nobody's that safe, not if they come annoying me they're not. You can do a lot to a man short of killing him. Alive can also mean not quite dead. As long as I leave your hands and your eyes, Leshkas isn't going to care slag for what happens to the rest of you."

So far as the eye could see the engineer was unmoved; and Shah found herself unaccountably reluctant to test his detachment from the inside. The memory of his mind was to her as the Ice Desert to a man with no compass. He said, "Lay a finger on me and it'll cost you Chad."

"A week ago I hadn't got Chad. And in three weeks I can strip it of everything I want. I've already told you it might be worth it to me to hear your scream."

"I don't scream," said Paul, so flatly it could have been true. "And Chad isn't all you'll lose if you try to pull this rabble you call an army out before they're satisfied. Have you ever seen a mutiny, Harry? It's like a wolf-pack when there's blood on the air: thousands of armed men, angry and frustrated, with nowhere to go and nothing to lose. The explosion of the human machine. I'd rather be me in your hands, Harry, than you in theirs."

Harry Jess had too much imagination to be a brave man, and too little education to accept that aspect of his make-up philosophically. He saw it as a weakness and could not contemplate it with equanimity. Switching the conversation unsubtly from that disturbing area he demanded petulantly, "Did you want something?"

"Yes. A monkey-wrench, three universal spanners, a book of logarithms, a bottle of drax and a pair of socks, size nine."

"And whatever makes you think —?" Harry began, amazed; then he stopped and a slow gloat spread across his pale thin face. "Did you say drax?"

"Indeed I did. A large, expensive bottle and I want it back."

Harry feigned horror. "I can't have a junkie fiddling around with my pile!"

Paul breathed hard and hung onto his temper. "Unless you replace that drax, soon, I shall not be fiddling around with it. I shall be curled up sweating in a corner while your pile blows its valves and you pack your bags."

Harry shook his head, his imitation sorrow too shallow to conceal delight at the development. "I've heard of it happening," he said sympathetically. "Some of the best brains mankind has produced rotted away by that vile stuff because they were arrogant enough to suppose they could control it. Tragic. Do you need some now, Paul? Can you feel the sweat beginning to break, the wonderful engineer's hands beginning to tremble? Cramps in the gut, shooting pains behind the eyes, and when you stop sleeping for fear of the nightmares they start coming in the daytime too? It's all right, Paul, don't be ashamed – I've heard all about it. Never experienced it, of course: we Northerners are a pragmatic lot, we can generally manage without seeking consolation in a bottle, but I'm sure life is hell for more sensitive types. Don't feel badly about it."

"I shan't," said Paul. "Until about this time tomorrow, at which point it will cease to matter that some barbarian gorilla has stolen my spanners because I shall be shaking too much to use them. Malaria, Harry. Sorry to disappoint you, but the only reason I use drax is because I'm allergic to quinine. If you can't find the thief you'd better find me an alternative supply: to the best of my knowledge the nearest nuclear engineer is a thousand miles south of here and can't stand the cold."

"How would I know where to find drax?"

"I don't care how," said Paul, rising to go. "Just do it."

Shah tasted his mind and decided the earl would welcome a suggestion. "Itzhak might know."

Harry looked at her vacantly, at the torque she was twisting in her hands. "Itzhak?"

"The poet. He does some doctoring. He might have some, or know where to get it."

"There you are then," said Harry expansively, waving a jewelled hand towards the door. "There's your answer. Go and see Itzhak."

# Chapter Three

After the palace fell to the Barbarians Itzhak, wandering, stumbled across the dove-grey cell remotely deep beneath the glittering staterooms. Windowless, under a low domed ceiling, the tiny vault was a little like a monk's cubicle and a little like a stone womb. Behind its shut door, his battery candle throwing calm shadows on the close walls, Itzhak felt instinctively safe; and since safety was the sensation he treasured above all others he immediately fetched down his belongings and staked his claim.

Shah led the way, her own candle registering their progress as a succession of architectural changes, always for the worse, as the plaster perfection of the upper levels gave way by degrees to older, rougher stones.

The man from the desert walked at her right shoulder, a little behind, half in shadow. Shah quickly recognised that this station, though possibly unconscious, was by no means arbitrary. He used other people as armour. In the unlikely event of Itzhak leaping out at them with a claymore, Paul's body would be shielded by that of the girl while his right arm remained free to wield his own weapon. Though he carried no sword and Shah could see no dagger, she found it difficult to believe that he habitually went defenceless. All his responses suggested otherwise.

They moved in silence. The stone walls listened greedily for any kind of sound to magnify and distort and throw back at them, but there was no sound, neither of conversation nor even footsteps: the girl wore slippers while her companion moved with the terse, elastic grace of a cat.

Shah could not have pin-pointed the moment at which she became aware of the crooked man. She was accustomed to having as a mental backdrop a mosaic of other minds, softly focused, a psychic hum; gradually as he drew closer to them his emerged from that background. She recognised him because she had seen him around the palace: his mind had a distinctive shape although it did not reflect that of his body. She knew he was a menial, though his mind suggested he had once been more than that, and she supposed he was on his way to some store or cellar.

Itzhak's cell was mazed about by tunnels but Shah never lost her way. It was a side-effect of her curious faculty – being able to home in on thoughts radiating from a human presence like ripples from a pebble tossed in a fountain.

Itzhak, behind his iron-hooped door, sounded startled at her knock. "Who's there? What do you want?"

"Shah," she called. "I want to come in. I have someone with me."

"Who? – Oh!" From the haste with which the bolt was drawn and the door flung back it was evident that his mind had gone first to Harry Jess. When Paul stepped out of the shadows the poet was torn between means that he had been mistaken and concern at confronting a stranger, an unknown quantity.

He was a tall man, of middle-age, slenderly built, somehow without substance. His skin was very pale and soft, his fine limp hair was white, his eyes were wide and pale blue. His effeminacy was so obvious that it drew no comment: the Northlanders were familiar with eunuchs. He had beautiful slim, strong hands.

Shah did not introduce them. She did not know quite how to. Also she was preoccupied with the other man, the one she had not seen but who she was now certain had followed them. When they entered Itzhak's cell he stopped and then edged forward again until he was just the other side of the dove-grey wall, close enough for her to step into his mind.

"He wants drax," Shah said without preamble, and without much attention either. "Harry – er – the earl said perhaps you could get him some."

"Drax?" echoed Itzhak, eying the stranger curiously. Itzhak's long narrow frame housed two distinct personnae, the spiritual considerably braver than the physical, so that, while his wide pale eyes were assessing Paul calmly, his mouth was babbling anxious, deferential nonsense. "Of course, lord. Only I don't think – it's not the sort of thing there's much – I'm sure I can find some though – er – Is it for you? I mean —"

Shah's gently probing psyche felt the mind beyond the wall unfold a flower as its owner, confident in his invisibility, concentrated on the proceedings within and on the poet's voice. Its portals open and undefended, she slipped into his mind like a practised bather entering water, with hardly a splash.

Several things happened virtually simultaneously.

Itzhak said, "Is it for you?"

Shah's eyes flew wide and she drew a sharp breath.

Paul, his own eyes locked on her face, shouted, "Lockwood, guard your thoughts!"

And Lockwood burst into the little room like a minor Act of God, knife in hand, totally uncomprehending and trying to fathom what action was required of him.

Paul slammed the door shut behind him and shot the bolt. "You damn fool," he snarled, "don't you trust me? Or do you think I need your protection?"

"I need to know what's happening," Lockwood returned stiffly, straightening as far as he was able. "I could see no reason for you to be brought down here, so I followed. Yes, it occurred to me you might require assistance: I was not aware you were invincible. And will you kindly moderate your language to such terms as may in chivalry be used between one gentleman and another?"

"Chivalry?" Scorn dripped from the word and turned to icicles under the influence of Paul's glacial rage. "My God, I don't wonder Harry Jess walked over you: I suppose you were still working out the protocol while he was chopping down your flag. And now your chivalry has made necessary the wanton destruction of perhaps the most remarkable mind in the world today. Damn you, Lockwood, damn your interference. You really are all I need: the fastest knife in the north, and brains like porridge. Well, don't just stand there gawping, finish what you started. Kill her."

Lockwood raised his blade, slowly, but made no move towards the girl. He looked confused and unhappy. "Kill her? Why? I don't understand you. She's only a girl. What did you mean – 'guard your thoughts'?"

"She's a telepath," Paul explained, his tone heavy with sarcasm. "A mind-reader. She knows what you were thinking. Lockwood – she knows."

Then he understood. His seamed face twisted with regret: only briefly, hardening as he moved towards her. Paul turned away, hiding the expression of loss condensing unexpectedly in his obsidian eyes.

As Lockwood's left hand closed on her wrist Shah said, very distinctly, "They have the prince."

For a moment the scene froze. Time took a breather. Then Itzhak's eyes grew enormous and terrified and he wailed, "Shah!"

Her mind was on the knife, her eyes on Paul, her reply – tense and brittle but without emotion – directed at Itzhak. "You always said you'd betray me to save yourself. Why should you expect any greater fidelity of me?"

Lockwood took a deep breath. "So I kill them both."

"If you kill Itzhak you won't get the drax," Shah said with that same flat urgency. "And if you go back to Harry Jess you'll have to explain what became of me." Paul turned back towards her and his brow, though creased with thought, was lighter; if he were not pleased then he was at least faintly impressed. "And then there's the other thing."

"Other thing?"

"You're a telepath too. You've been a long time in the desert. The kind of companionship I can give you, you can't pick up in every wayside tavern."

Paul's face that had started to clear, as if he were glad that she had made it difficult for him to kill her, went opaque again: again she touched that haunting sense of loss. "I'm not a telepath."

"Pardon my interfering once more," Lockwood said pointedly, flicking the edge of his knife with an impatient thumbnail, "but do you want these two dead or not?"

"Kill them," Paul said bleakly; then, with a weary sigh, "No, wait. She could be right. They could be more dangerous dead than alive."

"Knowing what they know, can we afford to let them live?"

"No, but then neither can I afford to kill them, at least not yet." He stared at Shah until the margins of her mind began to crawl with his scrutiny. Finally his eyes shifted to Itzhak. "All right. You: Can you get me that drax? – now, today?"

Itzhak was as pale as one of his vellums. His native mistrust of the world had been horribly reinforced; his recognition that his life was no longer in imminent danger gave him absolutely no confidence for the future. He thought desperately. "Yes, I – I think – Yes. Sir."

"Good. Well, apothecary, you've got a new apprentice – he can't reach the high shelves but he's useful with a scalpel." Lockwood grinned. Paul told him, "Watch him like a hawk. If he worries you, dispose of him. Otherwise get all the drax you can and bring it back here."

When they were left alone Shah thought philosophically, Here's where he loses all interest in my mind. But she was mistaken. Holding her in the searchlight gaze of those disturbing idol's eyes he said: "How long have you been Harry Jess's seer?"

"Seer?" She shook her long black hair. "I'm not his seer, or his prophet or his examiner or even his spy. I'm his whore."

In the months following her abduction, from a caravan as she travelled with her merchant brother to Gilgar, she had tormented herself with the word, made of it – for some reason she could not now quite recall – a flail for her own back; but with the passage of time both the word and the function it described became as familiar to her and as little uncomfortable as the hardness of the bed she slept on: it cost her no grief to say it.

Even so the engineer's reaction was disappointing. He merely raised one eyebrow and said, "It seems a waste of talent."

Stung by his indifference she replied tartly, "I'm alive, aren't I? With the exception of the one I gather you already know about, my predecessors aren't. They each died when they began to bore him. I have a distinct advantage: I know when he's getting bored before he does. A whore who can read her client's mind can just about guarantee satisfaction. It's a bit like screwing yourself," she added, deliberately crude, "but when the alternative is a quick trip to the chopping block you tend not to be too fastidious."

She could not interpret the look he gave her. There was no distaste in it, and no sympathy; interest, but not of a sexual kind; nothing to suggest that he could like her. Indeed, nothing she had seen of him so far suggested he could like anybody. His interest was calculating. "Does Harry know this?"

"Are you mad? Until you came along the only one who knew was Itzhak. Twenty-four hours after Harry finds out I'm dead. He'll think how he can use me, and then he'll think how I could use him, and then he'll get to wondering about all the things he's thought around me in the last three years. And finally the possibility of risk to himself will outweigh all the advantages and he'll have me killed. That's why your prince is quite safe from me. I couldn't reveal him without revealing myself, and that I am not prepared to do."

"And your poet friend?"

"Ah," said the girl softly. "Well, Itzhak is a very kind, very gentle person, who would never willingly harm anyone. But if he's frightened or hurt he'll do anything, say anything, betray anyone, to stop it. Your best defence so far as Itzhak is concerned is to keep him safely away from Harry. All the same, he's kept my secret for three years and it wasn't him who gave it away in the end."

She looked straight at Paul, her chin lifting, her luminous eyes fear-shadowed but resolute. She was afraid of him – more of him than of Harry – but her fear had weaknesses. When she had spoken to Paul of the desert she had spoken from experience. Her mind, extraordinarily gifted, craved the communion of like-oriented intellects. She had never known that glorious wordless intimacy, but knew that it existed and what form it must take from the shape of the emptiness in her soul. Sharvarim-besh was lonely.

And it was because her longing was greater than her fear that she demanded, "Why did you lie?"

Negligently he failed to meet her gaze. "Did I lie?"

"You said you weren't telepathic. Yet you read both my mind and your friend Lockwood's."

"No."

"Damn you," she cried in frustration, "what are you *talking* about? You knew Lockwood was there, you knew what he was thinking and you knew I knew. Of course you're a telepath."

"I recognised you as one the minute I saw you. You're not very subtle about it. You react too quickly. Sometimes you react to a thought that has no outward manifestation. Once I knew about you it was easy enough to spot you working. When you did it here, and were so startled by what you found, it had to be Lockwood, and there's only one thing on his mind."

"The same thing was in yours," challenged Shah. "Are you so sure it wasn't your mind I read?"

He grinned; his humour was more chilling than his threats. "Quite sure. You tried my mind once. You didn't like it very much. You didn't come again."

"There!" she exclaimed, over-triumphant in her effort to drown the icy spot of fear he conjured in her. "How else could you know that, except by some telepathic instinct?"

Faster than she could follow his sharp-edged mirth fled, his obsidian eyes iced over and the harsh planes of his face in a terrible hardness. His voice when it came was as bitter as the winter wind.

"I did not say I lacked the instinct, I said I had not the capability."

"Could you be a sort of latent telepath?" she ventured cautiously.

Paul's brimming fury flooded over, scalding Shah because she was nearest. "Damn you, woman, you cannot safeguard your own secrets but you're after mine as well! No, I am not a latent telepath. I was a latent telepath, and then I was a telepath, and now I am a former telepath. An ex-telepath. A telepath no longer."

Shah was deeply shocked, not so much by the pain she had finally wrung from him as by the implications for herself of what he had said. She had never considered, even momently, that her perception might be, independently of her, mortal. She whispered,

"How is that possible?"

Paul might have spared her then. His outburst had served its purpose, shattering her healing equilibrium and stemming her interrogation. He seldom so lost control of himself as to say or do something he had not intended, and that blind and heedless fury passed quickly. But below it lay a vast reservoir of molten anger, and it was his one indulgence that he vented it when and where the inclination took him without regard to common sense or common humanity. It was his second greatest weakness that he did not care about hurting people. His greatest weakness was that he thought this was a strength.

So he told her. "The people who had control of me grew afraid of what I could do. They had a psycho-surgeon burn it out of me with a laser."

Shah did not know what a psycho-surgeon was, nor a laser, but she knew subjectively what had been done to Paul and understood at last that faint, pervasive aura of bereavement. Vicariously she shared in it. Shah was a natural telepath, untrained, her faculty unsophisticated, its potential hardly scratched. Yet the prospect of life without it terrified her. Her perception was as essential to her, as fundamental a part of her, as her eyes and ears: deprived of that familiar, reassuring background of unconscious minds pursuing their daily rounds she would be blind and deaf. The world would lose its shape, its meaning, its certainty: she would have to wonder what people were thinking, what they expected of her, whether they meant her any harm. A vast area of her intellect would become an aching vacuum, incapable of being either filled or forgotten. Contemplation of such poverty sent deep shudders of pain and grief through her soul. Though she had never known another telepath, she had never for a moment considered herself without the gift. She considered now the possibility of losing it, as he had, to an act of premeditated violence, part mutilation, part rape.

Paul misunderstood the tears which started from her shocked eyes. He thought they were for him. "Save your pity for someone who needs it," he advised caustically. "Come."

31

When they returned to the poet's cell with a bottle of drax as big as the quite imaginary vessel Paul had described to Harry Jess, Lockwood and Itzhak found the prince in Itzhak's bed. Paul had carried him down while Shah scouted ahead a route from the tower to the dungeon.

Safely back in the basement Paul dumped his burden, somewhat unceremoniously, on the heaped cushions where Itzhak laid him down. The boy was wallowing on the rim of oblivion; possibly due to his condition, possibly because Paul hit him when he started to scream at imagined terrors in the kitchen remove.

Shah waited for the engineer to do or say something but she waited in vain: after depositing the boy he stood a moment, flexing his shoulder, then padded over to the door to check the dark tunnel beyond. Shah sighed and knelt beside the bed. Too old for lover, too young for mother, she began picking with distaste at the filthy rags of the young king's clothes.

But Itzhak, arriving home at that moment with the crooked man, shouldered her aside as with an inarticulate croon he dropped to his knees beside the hapless youth and folded long arms protectively around him.

Shah smiled up at Paul. "I think you've found your nurse." Paul was sneering but not any more than usual.

Paul told Lockwood how to administer the drug, how often, and what results he should expect. "Dosage at that level should keep him short enough that he feels it, not so short that he'll make up the difference himself. If he suddenly stops bothering, get me fast: it'll mean he's started synthesizing the stuff again."

"I wish you'd do it," muttered Lockwood, half a grumble, half a plea.

"I have to work on the pile or we'll have Harry Jess enquiring into my activities. The job will take me about a fortnight, then we leave. You won't get him fighting fit in that time but you should have him on his feet." Indicating the kneeling man ministering to the mumbling youth: "I don't think you'll have any trouble with our poet friend."

Lockwood nodded towards Shah. "What about her?"

"She's coming with me."

"Paul." The crooked man laid a hand on his arm as he turned away. "Don't bring Harry Jess down about our ears, not before the king is safe. After that if you want to come back for her, all right, I'll help you —"

Paul said quietly, "Do yourself two favours. Don't assume you know what I'm thinking: you don't. And don't make the mistake of supposing that this enterprise is in any way a democracy. You had your chance to save the prince and his father, and you blew it. Because of the strong possibility that you would I was paid to come here and pick up the pieces. You're not part of the solution, Lockwood, you're part of the problem. Do as I tell you and you may yet prove useful. But if you get in my way I'll deal with you as I would with anyone."

Lockwood was patently not accustomed to threats. His whole misshapen body stiffened and bristled; his creased face was a portrait of constraint. Finally he managed, "It's been said before."

Paul flashed him that brilliant feral grin. "Not by me, it hasn't."

# Chapter Four

Paul found Harry Jess at dinner, seated in splendid isolation at one end of the table where King John had entertained half the nobility of Chad. He had a succession of servants, awkward in borrowed livery, parade before him with dishes held high: so high that he had to crane to see what was on them. He was not too good on the details yet, but Harry was getting the taste for gracious living.

"You here again?" Harry enquired. "When are you going to fix this pile you insist I need?"

"I started today. Even engineers need to eat." Paul hooked out a chair with his foot and sat down beside a pyramid of fruit, helping himself to something yellow half way down.

"Soldiers, ostlers and those who maintain the public drains need to eat too, but they don't all do it here and at my expense. That passion-fruit has come something over a thousand miles."

"That passion-fruit is a banana, and if you want to try one sometime you have to peel it first." Paul demonstrated, throwing the discarded jacket carelessly onto the table.

Harry scowled. He was wearing an imaginative confection of ceremonial silk and brocade liberally laced with velvet, and about half the crown jewels; and he somehow contrived not to look absurd. "I suppose you want something," he said ungraciously. "You usually do. What is it this time?"

Paul said, "Will you sell me that girl of yours?"

"What girl?"

"The dark one. The southerner. Sharvarim-something."

Harry choked on his veal. "Shah? By all the gods, I don't know if you're a lion or a loon. Though I must admit, making an offer for her is preferable to theft. What's the matter? – another vacancy arisen in your friendly neighbourhood convent?"

Paul grinned. "You had no title to the other one: you abducted her and they wanted her back. So far as I know to the contrary you own this one; in any event, nobody's hired me to recover her. I'll pay you what she's worth."

"I don't want to sell Shah. She pleases me. But if it's a girl you want —"

"You've got it wrong again, Harry," interrupted the engineer. "It's not a lay I'm after, it's an assistant. With your genius for discrimination you've managed to kill off the entire maintenance crew of the pile. I'm interested in her hands: I've been looking for a pair that good for five years. You'll tire of her soon anyway, why not cash her in while you stand to make a profit?"

"I'm not tired of Shah," said the Barbarian thoughtfully. "No, Paul, she's not for sale – you'll have to keep looking."

Paul looked irritated. "All right. But I'm still going to need help with those valves. Lend her to me for a few days. In return I'll teach her how to run a check: it'll make your sojourn here a deal safer. They're pretty well fool-proof, these piles, they were designed to be operated by a handful of morons occasionally supervised by an idiot, but you're going to need someone in your household who can recognise a danger signal when she sees one."

Harry's narrow, intelligent face brightened. "Teach me."

"You?" Paul laughed out loud. "You've got hands like a pimp and you wouldn't do a thing I told you. If I can't borrow the girl I'll manage alone. But I can do a better job for you with her help."

Harry thought it over, examining the proposition for traps. There were obvious advantages in having close to him someone who understood something of his power-base, but one did not normally lend another man one's concubine, least of all a man who had made off with a previous incumbent. "All right," he agreed finally. "But you watch your step with her. She's mine."

"Fine," said Paul, rising.

"Does Shah know about this yet?"

Paul raised an eyebrow. "How should she know? She's a

mind-reader?"

Harry chuckled. "Perhaps she won't want to help you."

"Does it matter what she wants?"

The earl bellowed and Shah appeared, gliding across the marble flags with a rustle of variegated silk. Paul looked at her once, disinterestedly, then said to Harry, "She'll need something to wear."

Shah also looked at Harry, blankly, and the earl explained. "You don't mind, do you, Shah?"

"Not if it's what you want, my lord," she said tonelessly.

"Good, that's all settled then," said Harry. Beneath his bonhomie there glinted shards of malice. "Except for one thing, Paul. I know I've got a nasty suspicious mind, but it did occur to me after our last meeting that maybe you didn't need that drax for yourself at all, that maybe you weren't above selling it on the black market. Forgive me, I'm sure the suspicion is unwarranted, but perhaps you'd not object to setting my mind at rest?"

"How?"

"I'd like to see you take some of the stuff."

Shah's heart stopped, lurched and began to pound. Paul appeared unmoved. "You're a real little vampire, aren't you?"

Harry shrugged. "I'm responsible for what happens in this city. I need to know if someone is dealing in drax."

Paul glanced at the horologram above the door. "It's too early."

"Then we'll wait," Harry said silkily, settling back in his chair.

"All right, if it'll make you happy. But the least you can do if you're going to waste my evening is feed me."

Harry nodded. "You stay too, Shah. It'll be a chance for you two to get acquainted."

The meal was long and leisurely and the conversation easy. The men talked of the Ice Desert and the characters, more than half mythical, it had thrown up; they exchanged anecdotes of travel and tribulation, sniping and sharing a conspiratorial intimacy by turns. It occurred to Shah, excluded, observing with disbelief and deep foreboding, that they were closer in kind to one another than either was to anyone else. Of the meal she remembered nothing, not even if she ate. She could only wonder at Paul's self-control, that he could spend perhaps his last hour of sanity joking with the man about to render him mad. Clutching at straws, she asked herself if he could have some plan, but all hope was dispelled when he finally looked up at the horologram and said, "Well, I suppose I'd better give you your little treat and then we can all go to bed. I'll go and get —"

"No need," interrupted Harry, indecently eager, bringing a small purple vial from a chest under the window and laying it carefully on the table. Beside it he placed a slim wallet from which Paul, after a moment's pause, withdrew a hypodermic syringe.

He looked at it, and sniffed, and looked up at Harry. "I suppose these things are sterile?" All the humour had gone from his face and the familiar impassive curtain had dropped before it; but Shah, exploring round the edges, found thin shreds of anger, dismay and a peculiarly desolate resignation.

He took the syringe, drew off the purple fluid, made a tiny fountain of it in the air and punched it through the cloth of his trousers into his thigh where he discharged it. When it was empty he withdrew the needle and laid the syringe back on the table-top. "Happy now?"

Harry was torn between disappointment that his trap had not sprung and a small, obscene pleasure at what he had witnessed. If not happy he was at least satisfied. He nodded. "Like I say, I have a nasty suspicious mind."

Paul kicked back his chair and walked away. Shah half expected him to waver but he did not. At the door he paused with one hand on the frame and said shortly, "You'd better come while I fix you up with some proper clothes." Harry nodded again, and she had to fight against haste until she shut the door safely behind her.

Paul stumbled against her. "That bloody man!" he wrung out.

His face was white under the wind-tan, the eyes narrow and stretched, the jaw set; a muscle high up in his cheek worked as though he wrestled with an angel. "What can I do?" Shah whispered.

"A strip of that silk."

She had difficulty tearing it. Shakily she laughed. "I could do with Lockwood and his knife now." Paul drew one of the little secret darts, bodkin-slim, from his belt. Shah used the diamond tip to rend the fabric; then, in the act of returning it, remembered where she had seen its like before and froze. It was long seconds before she could drag her eyes from the silver dart to meet Paul's, but he was not looking at her. He seemed to be concentrating very hard and was barely aware of her. Shah took a deep breath and gathered her wits, and lodged the dart back in his belt and said, "What now?"

He tied the silk flag tightly round his leg above the puncture. When it was done he leaned back against the wall, panting slightly. "The next part I'd sooner not do in public."

His accommodation beside the powerhouse and Itzhak's cell in the basement were both too far and involved too many steps. Shah took him to her own room, only a shout away from Harry's, fully recognising the danger but considering that the risk of having him pass out on the floor of a busy corridor was probably greater. She steered him to a sedilla in the wall, then ran to bar the door and draw close the heavy curtains.

She turned back in time to see him slit open the cloth with the tip of a dart, drive its point into his leg where he had injected the drax, then wrench it viciously left and right. The blood leapt.

Shah, unprepared, gasped a little scream. Paul made no sound but vented a spastic breath through bared teeth. Shah rushed forward, tearing at her dress, but he would not let her stem the flowing blood. "Let it drain," he muttered, "I'd sooner cope with anaemia than drax." He allowed the bleeding to continue for some minutes, kneading the wound with his fingers to express the toxin, his eyes glinting darkly under lowered lids.

When he finally permitted her to dress the incision she bound it tightly with silk strips and then sat back on her heels. She said testily, because she had been frightened, "Would you care to explain that?"

Paul smiled thinly. Under the hooded lids the pupils of his eyes were enormous, the gold-flecked irises shining like the coronas of dark stars. He spoke deliberately. "I couldn't avoid taking the drug so I did the next best thing: made it work for its living. Give it pain to fight and it's effective and useful – it's when the narcotic effect is not balanced by a pain stimulus that it becomes destructive. Opening the injection site served two purposes: it washed out some of the drax held back by the tourniquet, and gave what was left something to work on. It may be a long night but I'll be all right tomorrow. Shall we be disturbed if we stay here?"

"You'll be safe enough," Shah answered obliquely. "I may have to leave for a short time but no one will come here."

"If I get too euphoric during the night you'll have to open the wound again," he remarked vaguely as the treacherous tranquillity lapped up around him and stole him into sleep.

To Shah's relief it did not happen. Nor did the call from Harry. Paul slept quietly through most of the night, isolated from discomfort by the drug cocoon, but as dawn wore close his rest grew fretful, fragmentary, and finally fractured as the drax in his bloodstream became too dilute to be effective. He woke stiff, sore, bad-tempered and patently not an addict.

While Paul was sweating drax out of his system in Shah's chamber, Edmund was sweating out the need for it levels below in Itzhak's. While Shah was watching Paul twitch and wondering if she should go for Lockwood, Lockwood was watching the king and wondering if he should summon Paul. His vigil was to last much the longer, to prove more harrowing than a battlefield, and to impress on him indelibly the debt he owed to the strange shrinking man with the hands of a surgeon and the devotion of a mother.

At first they hardly spoke except about their shared task, Lockwood being as uneasy of Itzhak as Itzhak was terrified of Lockwood. But as the hours passed and nothing happened, neither the peril of their position nor the anxiety each felt for the sick youth who was now King Edmund was sufficiently pressing to keep them from boredom. Lockwood asked, "Have you been long with the Barbarian?"

"I belonged to the old earl," said Itzhak. "Harry inherited me along with the title."

"Belonged?"

Itzhak smiled, that rare luminous smile that was made of the same stuff as his songs. "What, doesn't Chad understand the concept of slavery? Or is it that here only women are considered chattels to be bought and sold?"

Lockwood did not answer directly. A widower now for fifteen years, his own loved and loving wife had originally come to him by virtue not of mutual attraction and consent but of a bride-price. That he did not say as much was strange, because he had never considered it anything other than normal and proper. Instead he said, a little gruffly, "We have a peasant class."

"An entirely different thing," asserted Itzhak. "A peasant may labour under a multitude of feudal obligations but on the day-to-day level he is his own master and that makes him fundamentally a freeman. A slave may well enjoy greater comfort, he may eat better and sleep warmer; he may earn the confidence and consideration of people in the highest places; but he has no rights, no intrinsic human value. He is clay, and may be shaped or tramped upon.

"A peasantry grows out of the land. Your mastery of heated irrigation in Chad has given you agriculture, and slavery is an inefficient organ for pursuing it. Slaves need too much supervision, which in turn puts too great a strain on the yield potential of the land: too many mouths to be fed by too few hands. Chad needs a free peasantry. The Northlands don't. There is no agriculture. The economy is based on the caribou, which are owned by the lords and require little husbanding, and on brigandry. The Northlands have a nobility, a warrior class, and slaves."

Lockwood nodded, fighting back the notion that it was a thoroughly sensible way of arranging things. That came, of course, of being himself a warrior: he appreciated that others would feel differently. "Were you born a slave?"

"I wasn't born a Northlander," said Itzhak. "My family had a small isolated holding southeast of here, at the edge of the Ice Desert. I was acquired by the old earl in much the same way that Shah was by the new: stolen to decorate his halls. My parents had me sing for his pleasure when one of his expeditions brought him to our door. Well, he was pleased enough, I suppose, because when he left – with every beast of ours that could walk and every possession that was not nailed down – he took me too. I was nine years old. His musicians cut me for a castrato but they weren't as clever as they thought because after that my voice went bad. When they finally accepted that I wasn't just being difficult they let me write poetry instead."

"Will I have heard any of your rhymes?"

Itzhak laughed, a high light spritish chuckle like bird-song. "I hope you won't judge my talent by anything of mine you may have heard. It is my small revenge to write of Harry's triumphs in the worst verse I can construct. They please the earl well enough, as long as his exploits are sufficiently and flatteringly exaggerated he doesn't know enough of poetry to know that I mock him, but in civilised lands where my words tell Harry's tale they know, and they laugh."

Lockwood was impressed. He had not thought the pale man had so much spleen in him, to take a vengeance against his tyrant.

The time that dragged by for his keepers dripped like slow venom in Edmund's veins. The measured withdrawal had him in agony, made worse by enough gradually returning comprehension to understand that he must endure it, and with all possible quiet and dignity. Being a sixteen-year-old boy rather than an iron man, he did not wholly succeed.

In all his battle-strewn days, bloodstained and way-marked with death, Lockwood could recall nothing so harrowing as holding the writhing body of his young king, tied wrist and ankle lest in his anguished struggles he injure himself and gagged lest in the empty passages his screams carry too far, and knowing that he had inflicted this agony, and could stop it, and must not. At the height of the craving, before his body began to adjust to the reduced supply, the paroxysms lasted for an hour at a time, the possessed youth kicking and thrashing beyond any reasoned assessment of his physical capacity until finally even that unnatural strength was exhausted and he lay, still but for the tremors of his sobbing, in Lockwood's powerful arms while the gentle-hearted Itzhak wept openly and Lockwood inwardly.

# Chapter Five

Intimacy of a different kind was flowering at the pile. Different from the wary friendship growing in Itzhak's cell, quite different from the steamy manoeuvres suspicioned by Harry Jess; different almost certainly from any act of human intercourse then occurring anywhere in the world. Its singularity was due to the extraordinary intellects of the two participants, and it began with a man asleep over a book of logarithms.

Paul was not an habitual napper. Normally he slept only an hour or two during the stillest part of the night: if the need arose he could go for days without sleep with no marked lessening of efficiency, only an increasing tetchiness. But he had been working hard on the pile, the sealed room was warm and airless, perhaps there was still enough drax in his system to disturb his equilibrium. When he stopped in the middle of the day to split a flask of wine and a bowl of dust-free fruit with his assistant, he wedged himself in a comfortable corner with his feet up and the calculations reared against his knee, and gently fell asleep.

Shah's first instinct, when she saw what had happened, was to shake him awake in case Harry came calling. Then, defiantly, she supposed that a nuclear engineer was entitled to spend his lunchbreak as he chose and resolved to let him rest. She quietly removed the book from his lap and his glass from its perilous perch on his softly rising chest, then sat down at the bench to observe him in a way that, in his watchful wakefulness, she was inhibited from doing.

He was older than her and probably older than Harry but not by much: she put him in his early thirties. Awake he seemed older than that; asleep he looked younger. In sleep the deep harsh lines of his face, hardly less intractable than scars, softened and subtly changed, the anger and brittle bitterness leaching away. In their place Shah saw pain: the old underlying pain, not sharp but somnolent, enduring. The anger was an armour, partly to shield him from hurt but mostly so that the blood did not show.

Shah thought again of his terrible loss, a whole dimension ripped from his mind, and again failed to remain objective about it. Panic rose to suffocate her and she thought she must cry out, but a new notion came to divert her, at once impossible and compelling, and so strange that her fright faded.

It was this. Her mind was the same as Harry's and Itzhak's and Lockwood's except – it was of course a massive proviso – for her additional perception. Paul's mind was the same as hers except that his perception had been erased. So why was not Paul's mind the same as Harry's? – because it was not, nothing like, and nothing like any other she knew either. Could the ringing, windy plain echoing around that hive of industry be nothing more than the empty socket which had contained his inward eye? Or was his brain fundamentally different and his lost telepathy a camouflage – not the greatest but the least of his peculiarities?

And having thought that, she really had no choice but to go exploring. There would never be a better chance. Innocuous in sleep, his spare frame for once languorous and unstrung, his penetrating idol's eyes unseeing and still behind the lowered lids, his breathing unhurried, he might have been a laboratory animal anaesthetised for the experiment. Touching fingers as light as butterfly wings to the fine dark hair which spilt over his brow, she was struck by an unlooked-for vulnerability in his passive, haunted face and wondered about the last time this or something like it was done to him, his mind invaded not by another mind but by a tool which burned. Thinking that she was almost unable to continue, but curiosity and a practical need to know what she was dealing with over-rode conscience and she slid into his brain.

*He was still conscious which made it worse. The operation*

*would be impossible under anaesthesia, and there would be no pain, but it was as cruel as making a man witness the amputation of his arm or leg. A spinal injection had locked the skeletal muscles so that he remained quite still without restraint, a prisoner of his own body. As to the other, a neural suppressor protected those around him from telepathic assault, though the fruitless backwash of desperation occasionally sent trays of instruments clattering to the floor.*

*One of his governors sat beside him, absently patting his immobile hand and wishing he had some more meaningful comfort to offer, his heart – which was unaccustomed to doing much more than pumping – twisting uncomfortably while Paul begged for mercy as he had not before or since.*

*"You mustn't do this. Please – it's not too late. Stop them. I'll do what you want. Anything. You know what I'm capable of. With power like that you could command the world."*

*The old man nodded sadly. "I know. But what's more to the point, Paul, with power like that you could command the world, and neither I nor anyone else could stop you."*

*"All right, I appreciate that, I know why you're doing this. I tried to get away from you. Can't you understand why?"*

*"Of course I understand. I just can't risk it happening again. You're too dangerous, Paul."*

*"I am as you made me!"*

*"I know that. I'm sorry we didn't get it right. Perhaps after this we can give you more freedom, more happiness —"*

*"I don't want to be happy. I want to be whole! I'm not a congealed test-tube to be rinsed out and re-used, I'm a man. If you choose to make human experiments, you can't just flush away your mistakes. Besides, the experiment worked —"*

*"Yes. But the controls don't."*

*"You can't destroy me for wanting my liberty! Listen, it won't happen again, I give you my word —"*

*"Your word is worth nothing," the man said gently.*

*"You can't do this to me!"*

*Behind them another voice stated, "Ready." The man at his*

*side took Paul's hand in both of his and nodded.*

"No!"

*They said there would be no pain. No pain?! – what then did they call this, this piercing wrenching rending dismemberment in his head, like being eaten alive? He moaned aloud, and felt the hands tighten on his own. Agony dimming his eyes he whispered, "Kill me."*

*"That would be murder."*

*"So – is – this."*

*"You won't always feel that way," said the old man kindly. But he did.*

She had known before opening her eyes where she was, if not why. That deep cutting chill and the white glare which pierced even shuttered eyelids were unmistakable. The Ice Desert was not so much an environment as an element: it surrounded the cities of the northern world, lapping against their walls, exquisite and pristine and eternally threatening to flatten the walls and flow back over the cities. When the desert winds blew long and hard the ice crystals would pile up in great drifts along the windward walls, and the people of the cities would venture out when the wind stopped to gaze in awe at the white ramps like highways into their fortresses, and would bury their sense of menace under uneasy jokes until labouring teams lowered the frozen wave which dwarfed their defences and made their entire way of life seem fragile and transient. From the standpoint of men, the Ice Desert was like time itself.

Shah was not initially alarmed so much as confused. She could not remember how she came to be outside the city. But Chad could not be far and its walls were high in the flat silver plain, and its remarkable fields stretched wide into the ringing wastes. When her eyes cleared fields or ramparts would loom close.

When her eyes cleared what she saw was more whiteness. Turning on the spot again and again she saw no city, no towers, no fields; no concrete water-pipes haloed with languid steam, no labouring peasants, no patrols; no men, no beasts. All she saw was the Ice Desert, eternal, immutable, under the silver sky. It was all there was to see. Even so she did not finally believe it until she turned her mind upon that mosaic background of other people's thoughts and could not find any.

At the hearts of galaxies, where every planet is washed by the light of multiple suns, night never falls and darkness is the great unknown. To Shah, bathed since birth in the radiance of multiple personalities, the great unknown was solitude. Now it smote her like a blow, sending shockwaves rippling through her, rooting her to the frozen ground. Childish in her desolation, she clasped her arms about her trembling body and, to fend off hysteria, concentrated all her efforts in an intense search.

And indeed there was something there; not a pattern of minds but perhaps a mind, expansive but tenuous like an ocean inches deep, or like the machine noise at the powerhouse, so deep and regular and constant that you had to really listen to hear it at all. Now she was attuned to it the pulse seemed all around her, but it had direction too, like the desert wind which is everywhere but originates elsewhere. She still did not know what it was, if it was in Chad, even if it was human, but because it was the only dimension in an otherwise featureless environment, and because if she did not do something soon she would literally die of inaction, Shah focused on what seemed to be the heart of the beat and began to walk.

Time in these high northern latitudes, where through the short summer the sun circled barely perceptibly below the horizon, was difficult to judge. Chilled to the marrow in her inadequate clothes she trudged through the glaring day, so blue-cold that the tundra itself seemed hardly colder, so weary she walked in a miserable dream, lost and deeply frightened. Only the subliminal psychic heartbeat stood between her and madness, kept her walking away from death.

She was roused from her reverie of despair by two possibly unconnected changes. The first that she noticed was a sudden quickening of the mental beam, a strengthening of both intensity and activity, like opening the door on the powerhouse and transforming the dull hum into a dozen different busy machine-sounds. Also, the temperature was rising. Looking up, she

46

found the plain ahead ended abruptly in a glass curtain.

Approaching, cautiously but with a lightness of step borne of relief that this penance of a place was not after all unending, she recognised that the curtain was not in fact glass but, like everything else in the northern desert, ice. It hung in shimmering folds from half way up the sky, static as ice but dancing with the lights of some internal, intrinsic life. Shah touched it carefully and it was as cold as ice, yet she perceived a heat-source somewhere behind it. The curtain, being rigid ice, made no sound, but sound was all around, out at the limits of her hearing, strange and secret yet somehow not sinister, as if she knew it, knew it all, if only she could remember. . . .

The curtain had convolutions in its serpentine shape where the folds folded back on one another. Seeking the sound, and the psyche, but more than either of them the promise of warmth, Shah passed through one such gap into

"You're all right now. Come on. Wake up, damn you." He sounded as exhausted as she felt, but his voice finally brought some semblance of intelligence into her blank, stretched eyes and she looked at him with perplexity, perhaps an aftermath of shock, but with a soul that was recognisably her own.

Paul slumped to the floor beside her, wondering if she was aware yet of the dark marks of his hands on her cheeks, wondering if she felt any more mentally and physically battered than he did. Later, when they had both recovered somewhat, he would be brilliantly, devastatingly angry, but just now he lacked the energy. It occurred to him briefly that if Harry should chance upon them sprawled like this, so evidently spent, he would leap to a conclusion almost more dangerous than the truth; but Harry was a bridge he would have to cross sooner or later and anyway he was too tired to care.

"Paul?" His name felt strange on her lips, like saying her own. When he did not respond she tried again, tentatively, full of an apprehension she could not explain.

"Yeah." Spreadeagled beside her, he lay with peculiarly graceful

47

abandon, his eyes closed.

"I feel – awful."

"Serve you bloody well right."

"Please – what happened?"

Paul rolled his head towards her. She had sat up and was hunched over her bent knees, cradling her head in her arms. She sounded close to tears.

"You made a mistake. You tried exercising your talents inside my head. You got lost."

Shah, remembering, experienced a surge of panic and bit back a scream. "Gods! Paul, it was – cold!"

"What did you expect," he snarled, "a welcome mat and a log fire? What were you thinking of?"

"I'm sorry, I didn't mean – I only – I wanted to know about you. Please don't be angry."

Paul looked away. "Forget it."

"I don't understand. I've been tripping in and out of people's minds all my life. Nobody's ever known before. I never guessed I could hurt anyone."

His temper snapped. "I'm not anyone," he spat. "I'm not like you, I'm not like your Barbarian friends, I'm not like anybody you know about. You think your party-tricks amount to something special? When my brain was intact I had a perception compared with which yours is fog-bound; I was telekinetic and there was every indication that teleportation lay within my grasp. You don't even know what those things are, do you? You're a paranormal midget. What do you know about telepathy?"

"Enough to know," she cried, "that if I were you and I met me, I wouldn't let envy keep me from passing on secrets that were no longer any use to me."

Pain stabbed in his eyes; he swung, she flinched; his open hand struck into her bruised cheek with a crack like thin ice. The blow changed everything. A pettiness, it left Paul frozen, his arm awkwardly raised, a slow tide of humiliation rising through him. He abhorred physical contact, avoided it obsessively, so that slapping Shah out of her catalepsy had required an effort of will. Now he had struck her again, in wrath, and he felt like an animal.

Shah was less shocked by his violence than Paul was. His abandonment under provocation of intellectual superiority in favour of physical dominance was a human act, something she understood better than the torrents of clever, angry words which poured from him and over the top of her head. Yet she could have wished the favour unasked. She had no right to make demands of him: she was nothing to him, he owed her no thing save one night's sanctuary and a few strips of silk.

Paul was struggling, against the conditioning of a lifetime, with the inexplicable urge to apologise. Looking neither at her nor away, sullen with discomfort, he finally wrung out, "That was unnecessary."

It was not the most eloquent apology Shah had ever heard, though it might have cost the most. A man to whom efficiency was more a god than a goal, she doubted if there was a word in his vocabulary more loaded with calumny. She would have smiled at his dismay but for the certainty of wounding him further. Instead she said quietly, "I had no right. I had no right to trespass in your mind, and I had no right to say what I did. Could we perhaps forgive one another?"

After a moment he nodded, turning away.

Shah said, "How did I get out?"

"I fetched you."

She smiled. "Just like that?"

"No, not just like that," he snapped, rounding on her, ready for anger; then he saw her smile and slowly answered it with a crumpled one of his own. "No," he said again, more softly. "Not just like that. I don't know what would have happened to us, you and I, if you'd had to stay in there, but we damn nearly found out."

When he felt, with shock, outrage and a deep foreboding, the wormish sensation of another personality in his mind Paul was instantly awake and tried to rouse Shah, without success. She sat sagelike, still and open-eyed and quite impervious. In desperation he clawed at his head, as if he could scratch her from his brain. Then, with the nausea sweeping through his synapses and the pain they said he could not feel shooting down the nerve chains, yielding

49

up all hope of an early relief, he let his useless body collapse in a twitching faint and, quiet as despair, followed her inside.

"Why did you go so *deep?*"

"I was lost," she explained patiently. "I didn't know where I was. I thought I was in the desert. I was freezing to death: I had to find some shelter."

"But why that way?"

"I seemed to hear someone calling."

Paul too hesitated at the glass curtain, that emotional thermocline which served to protect his innermost ego from a hostile world, and vice versa. But he knew Shah had passed that way from the damage she had done, and from the turbulence within welling to counter the invasion. Whether his brain could produce antibodies, actual or psychological, to deal with the intruder he had no way of knowing, but he was quite sure that Shah would not leave alone and so – reluctantly, shrinking from the almost incestuous contact – he slunk into that roiling region whence all his passion originated.

There was a hollowness in his eyes as they faced one another across the service chamber of Harry Jess's nuclear pile. No anger, no pain, nothing: an awful nothing, a pit of self-knowledge. He had made a journey such as no man had made in the history of the world, a voyage no man should have had to make, and though he had both survived and succeeded he had traversed a realm the human mind is not equipped to travel and the experience had marked him.

Shah said, "I owe you my soul. Was it very bad?"

To be rejected as a foreign body by your own brain; to be smothered and buffeted, and raged at by a defence mechanism which was never designed to discriminate between inimical and benign trespasses; to feel your strength sapping and your concentration tear under the bombardment, knowing that only strength and concentration stand between you and dissolution; to have to press on when all your instincts, every natural and acquired sense urges you, pleads with you, screams at you to turn and flee, to run as far as you can as fast as you can because no girl ever born was worth this mayhem at once in you and around you; that was bad. But it was private, and anyway incommunicable. He managed a slow, crooked grin, "Not bad," he said. "Just a bit like screwing yourself."

Later, after they had rested, with his arms plunged into the entrails of the machine, Paul said in a low voice, "I'll teach you, if that's what you want."

Shah stopped, looking at him. "What?"

"What I can. What I can remember. It'll be rather like a paraplegic teaching ballet, it's a long time since I've been able to practise and I can't demonstrate. You'll have a rotten time: I've never taught anybody anything before, I've no reason to suppose I have a vocation for it, I shall probably work you unreasonably and shout a lot. But you ought to get some training, a talent for telepathy is too special to go to waste, and if I don't coach you I don't suppose there's anyone else who will."

"I've hurt you so much already," whispered Shah.

Paul glared at her and demanded roughly, "Is that no?"

"Oh no," she replied fervently. "No, that's yes please, you'd better believe it, when do we start?"

"Now," he said grimly. "Before I lose my nerve."

He was right about one thing: he had no vocation for teaching. He had no patience. He expected her to be able to produce an effect in about the time it took him to describe it, speaking fast and using words she only half understood. He made no allowance for her lack of sophistication, or the fact that – never having shared her facility – she had not the vocabulary to deal with its uses and nuances. He treated her a little like a machine and a little like a mentally defective child; he drove her, ox-like, with the goad of his scorn, unrelentingly, until her brain crawled with exhaustion, so that she escaped from him at the end of each day with relief so profound that Harry Jess's demands were positively welcome by contrast. Yet she was happy. For the first time in her adult life she was doing what she wanted to do; someone whose opinion she valued treated her – however brusquely – as something worthwhile; and she saw, or rather felt, like a quickening in the air, a prospect of escape. It was a measure of her euphoria that she had all but forgotten, in her new-found relish for the future, the very real and present danger posed by the secret in which she shared.

She might have worried more if Paul had allowed her the time. He did not. He worked her every moment they were together, either on the pile or on her developing faculties; not infrequently he expected her hands to be engaged on the one task and her mind on the other. Much that he had her doing she did not understand: some of it seemed to have remarkably little value, and some she was already familiar with and mistress of – only he insisted she learn it again his way. As the days passed in the close confines and rancour of the pile, Shah felt her brain stretching.

Paul set her deceptively simple exercises. "Find Harry." As she moved obediently towards the door he blew up with overstrained patience and frustration, reminding her that his task was more alien to him than was hers to her. "Dear God, is it a dog I'm training? Where are you *going*? You can find Harry with your feet nailed to the floor. Use your head, woman! It's just my luck," he snarled despairingly, "I finally find a telepath and not only is it female but she's got sawdust between her ears."

When he had finished Shah said, "The throneroom."

"What?"

"Harry. He's in the throneroom."

Paul breathed heavily. "Right. Alone?"

Shah considered. "No-o-o —"

"Who's there?"

"Soldiers. And – others."

"Stay with Harry. What's he thinking about?"

The projection of her mind, that she had learned to shape and motivate, went through the stone passages like a ferret. She pushed it out with the front of her brain, with a near physical effort that hurt the muscles of her eyes. Unseen and unsuspected, it quested like a ferret for the scent of its quarry, quickening to a familiar resonance. From the anteroom her projection recognised that Harry Jess was upon his purloined throne. Passing through the closed door it homed in on him, aware of an animated background of other minds, some of them known to her, but concentrating on its target. Infiltrating Harry's mind it saw the small assembly with his eyes, heard its babble with his ears, felt the surging triumph in his breast and tasted the sweetness of vengeance in his mouth.

Shah frowned. "I don't understand. What is a blood eagle?"

Paul knew. He knew not only what it was but also what it meant, that she asked that question now. His face tightened and went hard and the gold flecks flashed in his narrowed eyes, but before she took in his strange expression and before he had chance to explain she found the answer in Harry's sadistic mind. Accustomed as she was to the Barbarian's thoughts, this one rocked her. The appalling vision burning in her brain, she turned her face ghost-white to Paul, struggling for words. Her voice was a shocked whisper.

"He knows about the prince. Paul, he knows everything! They're all there, in the throneroom: the prince, and Lockwood, and poor Itzhak. He means to kill them all, but the prince – the prince —"
She could not finish.

"I know," grunted Paul. "The Blood-Eagle."

# Chapter Six

In one sense Harry Jess was hardly a Barbarian at all. In the first place he was literate. In the second he thought too much, studied too much, paid too much heed to the past and to the future. In another and very real sense the title fitted him like a glove, because mostly what he thought about, studied and paid heed to was cruelty.

Familiarity with his people's history had given him the Blood-Eagle. Its charm for Harry lay not only in its cruelty but also in its baroque selectivity. It was specifically a death for conquered kings. He would have used it for John if he had remembered in time. Now he could employ it on his son and heir. Harry did not suppose a king had to be crowned to qualify: it should be enough that an heir apparent outlive his royal predecessor; anyway, Harry made the rules now.

Because of the pleasure the Barbarian anticipated deriving from him, Harry regarded the doomed youth almost kindly, finding it in himself to admire defiance from a boy who could barely stand without assistance. A sick sweat filmed his pallid face, and the flesh had wasted from his frame so that blue shadows played between his ribs beneath his rent shirt. Yet he was not altogether unimpressive. If there was fear in his fevered eyes, there was also contempt. His frail body bent from illness, not abjection. Harry thought he would make a good enough death despite his scant years, pegged out in the square with his chest prised open and his lungs spread on the cobbles either side like eagles' wings.

Nor was he disappointed in Lockwood. He had of course heard of the hunchback who commanded the Chad army: now he saw him Harry could not understand how the man had passed so long unrecognised. He remembered his first intelligences of this cripple, received with amused incredulity back in the chill halls of his Northlands when he began to plot his invasion. He had thought then that either the reports were exaggerated or Chad was idiot-led. Now he could see for himself that Lockwood was indeed extremely crooked; still as an adversary he had proved worthy. Losing his military campaign he had switched to guerrilla activity under the very noses of the new garrison. On his eventual discovery – by the random chance of a soldier with toothache being hustled along to the poet-healer by half a dozen colleagues – it had taken the entire patrol to subdue him: two men had fallen to his knife before the others succeeded in securing his murderous hands to a yoke across his shoulders, by the entirely reasonable expedient of first beating him senseless. He appeared before Harry Jess crucified, hung about with chains and groggy from the blows he had sustained; and Harry still had to fight back an impulse to keep large pieces of furniture between himself and the cripple.

His respect, however academic, did not extend to his own poet. Itzhak cowered before him, his mouth flapping like a flag in a gale and small terrified sounds and gushing half-formed apologies coming out by turns. Harry thought he had never seen a more disgusting sight and wanted to kick the gaping white face unrecognisable. Then he thought he could do better than that. He would kill Itzhak first, for the pleasure of his panic; then the boy; then, with the reason for his living smeared across the cobbles outside, Lockwood.

But not yet. First there was the question of coconspirators to be resolved. The gibbering poet was an obvious candidate for the inquisition, but when at a sign from Harry two of his guards laid meaty hands on him Itzhak breathed a tiny shriek, his head rolled back and he was limp in their grasp.

The men exchanged incredulous looks over the slack figure. "He's fainted."

"What?" Harry leaned forward, menace giving way to irritation.

"Fainted, my lord. Dead to the world." They hefted him experimentally. "We never even started!"

"Ye gods, there's no backbone in the entire world outside the

Northlands," declared Harry. "Any of my men," he told Edmund, "would suffer torture in total silence for me."

"Those whose duties involve listening to you," retorted the king, "do."

Harry's pale eyes kindled. "Oh ho, a humorist. Round here, sonny, I make the jokes. The only ones it's safe to laugh at, anyway. And for gods' sake, stand up straight. Your father was as straight as an arrow after five days with these two." The guards winced, unhappy to have their failure resurrected.

The boy drew himself up with more courage than strength and said proudly, "I need no lessons in deportment from a Barbarian brigand with the morals of a stray cur. Nor do I need your assurance that my royal father died like a king."

"Don't be jealous," Harry said, very softly. "You too shall have a king's death. Only, before that, you will tell me who aided you."

Edmund's lip curled and his chin jutted. It was, Harry recalled with interest, the exact expression with which King John had greeted his enquiries. Something of an upstart himself, Harry had an eye for tradition.

Lockwood said, "King Edmund is his father's son and my student. He will tell you nothing."

"In that case," replied Harry, rising smoothly from the throne and rounding on the crooked man, "before he dies you will tell me who gave him succour. Everything I know about you, Lockwood, assures me that such betrayal lies entirely outside your nature and ethics. Yet you will do this alien thing because no one in the world means anything to you beside this weakly youth, no one's sufferings are of any weight beside his, and you will sell anyone's soul – as you would sell your own – to save him hurt. Ah Lockwood, with devotion like yours behind me I could rule half the world!"

Edmund said, "All you have behind you, Harry Jess, is an army of bullies, compounded by thuggery and motivated by greed. One day soon one of them will put a knife in your back. All you'll rule then will be six feet or rather less of the tundra, if anybody cares enough to bury you."

"And to bury you, sonny, they'll have to scrape you up with a shovel," snapped Harry. "Lockwood, name those who aided you or your pretty prince begins the long slow business of dying now, here in this room. There's a fire in the hearth whose use should not prove beyond the scope of an inventive mind."

The king let his eyes travel slowly round the room from which his murdered father had ruled his broken city. When they fell on Lockwood he smiled; when they reached Harry they fixed him coolly. "You see before you those who served me: Lockwood, gladly, because he is my gallant friend and first noble, and Itzhak, against his will, because Lockwood would have killed him else. None other."

Harry, noting that Itzhak had revived enough to listen approvingly to this speech, kicked the prostrate poet. "Is this true?"

"Yes – yes, lord, utterly true," Itzhak agreed fervently, "he had a knife and would have killed me; naught else could induce me to deny my lord – my gracious lord —" He had hold of Harry's foot and was trying to kiss it.

Harry snatched it back with difficulty and some loss of dignity. "No, fool. That no others were involved?"

"Yes," nodded Itzhak, peering anxiously up at the earl's angry face. "No? What does my lord wish to hear? No! No, it's a lie, there were others. Many others, scores, hundreds —"

"I want the truth, you cretin," yelled Harry. "I shall have it. My fire is a democratic element: it will burn a poet as well as a prince."

Itzhak squawked and tried to grovel still lower, which was impossible; the sergeant of the guard, at a sign from Harry, moved towards the hearth, pulling on a glove deliberately; and nicely on cue Paul shouldered open the door and shouted across the room to Harry Jess, "Are you busy?"

Every sound in the chamber ceased; every eye in the chamber turned on him. It was an effect he rather enjoyed creating, but there was not time to relish it long. "I see you are. Still, my business is more important than theirs."

"You've done it again," fumed Harry. "Look, I'm not going to tell you any more. You want to see me, you *ask* – and you *wait* until it suits me to grant you an audience. This is my city now."

"Not for long, it isn't. Somewhere along the line, Harry, you've managed to upset a clever man, as a result of which you're going to lose your city, most of your subjects, half your army and quite possibly your life."

The silence stretched until it crawled. Harry broke it. "What are you talking about?"

Paul's eyebrows twitched a little facial shrug. "When I closed up the pile last night it was fine. When I opened it this morning it had been tampered with. It's taken me till now to work out what he did. Nothing crude from this lad, no bashing it with a sledgehammer. He knew his way around. He's disconnected the – oh well, you wouldn't understand, but the point is that there is now no way to prevent the pile blowing the Garden City of Chad into a cloud of dust and small pebbles three miles high. I've managed to slow the process down to give you something over four hours to organise an evacuation. Alternately, leave someone else to organise it, find yourself a fast horse and ride the devil into the wind. That's what I propose to do." He turned back to the door.

"Wait." The terse authority in Harry Jess's voice brought Paul to a halt with a jerk that rather surprised him, though it was what he both expected and required. "Do you mean to tell me I'm going to lose Chad because of this damn pile of yours?"

Paul snorted. "It's not my pile, it's yours. In view of the lengths you went to to acquire it, it's a pity you didn't guard it better. His father kept it safer than a favourite concubine."

Harry looked where he was looking and, startled, back again. "You know the boy?"

"Of course. That's Prince Edmund – King Edmund now, I suppose, for all the good it'll do him. And that's Lockwood. Was he anywhere near the pile last night?"

Lockwood, who had listened with increasing agitation to the exchange, could contain his wrath no longer. "You devil," he exploded, struggling with the rod across his back so that his attendants shuffled around him uneasily, "you worthless, ignoble, treacherous devil!"

"Shut up!" screamed Harry. He was shaking on his feet and it was hard to say whether fear or fury had the upper hand. "My city's about to blow up and you stand there calling one another names? Cripple, is this your doing?"

Lockwood made a visible effort to master his temper, dragging homicidal eyes away from Paul with difficulty. "Given the opportunity to blow something up, Barbarian," he said in a low voice, "I should have chosen you, not a city of twenty thousand people most of whom I have know all their lives."

Paul shrugged. "Well," he said off-handedly, "I can't think of anyone else and quite honestly, I feel the topic would be better discussed on the far side of a mountain some three hours' ride from here. Will your sergeant raise the alarm or shall I? The more warning your soldiers get the more army you'll have left to play invasions with when the smoke clears. There's always another city."

"You're going nowhere," snapped Harry; which the sergeant, who had been growing increasingly restless, chose to interpret as a direction to himself. Saluting smartly, he wheeled and went. That, Paul noted with satisfaction, reduced the ungodly to the earl, the double act which had frightened Itzhak into a dead faint, and a couple of rather junior hoodlums by the door. A bit more stirring, he thought, and they too would melt away; and no one would come back once the word was out.

While Paul was indulging in a cautious gloat, Harry Jess was prowling the throneroom like a frustrated cat. He was, Paul decided, furious rather than afraid. He was an undoubted coward, even a celebrated one, but somehow this massive threat had failed to get through to him. It was as if he simply could not believe that, having got what he had wanted for so long, he could lose it so quickly. Instead of leading the exodus, he was fretting about the coincidence of timing: ultimate victory over the Chad royal family one minute, prophesies of total doom from this ubiquitous engineer the next. Experience on both sides of the arras had taught Harry that coincidence was more usually conspiracy.

Watching Paul slit-eyed and sideways he enquired, "Did you know the boy was still here?"

"It was a reasonable assumption," Paul returned idly.

"Did you know where he was?"

"If I'd been looking for him, I'd have started in the palace."

"Why didn't you *tell* me?"

"I'm a nuclear engineer, Harry. You're the general of the occupying army. I assumed you knew your job."

"Treacherous," Harry said, thoughtfully and apparently without cause. He went on prowling.

Paul frowned. He did not like not understanding. He also did not like the time this was taking. "I really am getting rather nervous," he remarked. "I'm ready to go. I came to warn you: I wasn't prepared for a full-scale debate."

Harry stopped pacing and looked him in the eye, and there was more intelligence in the look than Paul would have chosen. He thought of Shah and he thought hard.

"You're not leaving this room," said Harry, "until I comprehend what part you have played in all this."

"You've no more time for conundrums than I have," advised Paul. "Anybody who's not on his way out of this city in the next half hour has palpably little chance of survival. Chad is a bomb. The city and those left in it will not exist for more than four hours. Those closest to the explosion will be vaporised; they will disappear. A little further away they'll be burned to carbon. Further away again they may survive the blast but die, after varying periods of time and from assorted effects, as a result of exposure to heat and/or radiation. We have to leave, Harry. Kill these if you want but let's get out of here."

Lockwood lurched again, wordlessly but with such determination that the two guards by him had to hold like grim anchors and Paul fell back apace. Lockwood was not acting.

Harry was still looking thoughtful. "It's funny how much he resents you. Any idea why?"

"None," Paul said coldly.

"Treacherous," Harry said again. His voice was as softly dangerous as new snow on a glacier. "An odd word to use. A term not of abuse but of censure. Treachery is an act against duty, or friendship. And yet he's a literate man, you wouldn't expect him to use words loosely."

Paul made no reply, seemed hardly to listen. Harry smiled slightly, hungrily, as he warmed to his theory. "So perhaps he didn't. Perhaps he had a right to expect from you better than he got." He chuckled, watching Paul impishly; then, denied a reaction, laughed out loud, immoderately, with every appearance of delight. "Dear me," he said moistly, climbing into his throne, "I don't know what it is about you that arouses my nasty suspicious mind. But it would explain certain things if we assumed a community of interest between these people and you. Each of them is known to you. Two of them you have worked for in the past, the third supplied you with the drax I never quite believed you needed. Malaria isn't that common in the Ice Desert. The boy's a much more likely candidate for a junkie. And you have this almost uncanny knack of turning up at interesting moments."

"I read minds," Paul said, deadpan.

Harry grinned. "No, what you do is spy. And if you're a spy, and if your intention is to extract this feeble princeling from my evil clutches, then the panic about the pile is a diversionary tactic and Chad is likely to last for a thousand years. You, on the other hand, are unlikely to last more than a very few days. But they'll be long ones."

Paul's voice was flat, passionless and deeply convincing. "That pile has gone critical. It will explode. Chad will be destroyed, and those who delay leaving will without any shadow of a doubt die. Unless you want a full-scale mutiny, order your men out now."

Afterwards Harry could never describe exactly what happened to him. He started to respond, scornfully, in the negative, when a kind of fog got into his brain and clogged it up and stopped him from seeing what he was doing and hearing what he said. It did not hurt and there was nothing to be frightened of, but when the fog receded and he rediscovered himself sitting on his throne with his head against the padded back he found it had left an icy spot of fear, a chill, in his heart.

The soldiers were gone. Lockwood, unchained, was rubbing life back into his arms and watching him with a kind of black triumph.

The boy was slumped on the window-seat, looking out over the square. Itzhak was blowing his nose, loudly and wetly, on a silk flag of a handkerchief. Near the door Paul and the girl Shah, whom he did not remember arriving, were deep in quiet, angry conversation. Apart from Lockwood's murderous stare, no one was paying him any attention, which the Earl of the Northlands found very strange.

"What the hell —" His voice came out a thin treble; Harry coughed it down and started again. "What the *hell* is going on here?"

Paul looked up with an air of distraction, frowned and returned to his confab. "Not now, Harry." It was the most cutting remark the earl had ever heard.

"Please," said Lockwood, never taking his eyes off the hunched, defensive figure on the throne. "Please, Paul – can't I have him? I'd be forever in your debt."

"If you live you'll be forever in my debt," Paul said shortly.

"For the king," Lockwood said, swallowing. "I owe him vengeance. It won't take long."

"No."

"Why *not?*"

"Because," snarled Paul, rounding on him, "if you ever stop arguing, and if she ever stops arguing, Shah is going to take you down to the mews and using my camels you're going to escort this king-thing out of here. To enable you to do this in some degree of safety, I propose to stay behind for a short while with a sharp knife at the gullet of this other megalomaniac. As I am not optimistic enough to try holding a corpse hostage, it follows that I require Harry alive until I'm ready to leave."

Harry shouted: "When my men get back here —"

"They're not coming back. They're saddling their horses and packing their spoils, and thanking whatever gods they pray to that you sent them away before the urge to join the exodus made them run out on you."

"I —?" Harry almost choked on his own indignation. "I did *not* send them away. I did not."

"You think they went because I asked them politely?"

Shah was watching Harry's eyes and feeling his distress. Not just the physical fear of being alone and defenceless in a room with five people each having good reasons to kill him, but the mental panic of being unable to account for himself. She remembered the pain he had given her, and the shame, and also the long nights that might have been lonely without him snoring softly beside her, face down, one arm flung across her waist. With surprise she realised she no longer wanted retribution.

Harry cringed as she approached him. He had heard women could be the worst they were more inventive, and less scrupulous. But when she stopped and gazed into his face he saw no hatred in her jewel-dark eyes, only something akin to compassion, which he did not understand.

She said simply, without pride, as a statement of fact: "I made you do it. I got into your mind and made you dismiss them."

"You – my mind —?" stammered Harry, chalk-faced. "How?"

"I'm a telepath, I read minds. I've been reading yours for three years. This other thing I didn't know if I could do until today. Paul taught me."

Harry shrank further into the throne; he looked stricken.

Lockwood said, with conviction but to no one in particular, "I said he was a magician."

When they had gone, so quietly and carefully that they must have aroused suspicion but for the chaos outside, Harry found something to say but Paul silenced him with a raised hand. Positioning himself at the window he concentrated, as intently as keeping an eye on his hostage would permit, on the clamour and bustle in the square. But no particular hue-and-cry elevated itself above the general mêlée and in due course four figures, swathed in furs and hooded for the desert, with two laden camels and a skittish, leggy calf, crossed the cobbled expanse from the palace compound to the west gate. The great portal stood open and unguarded. The small camel train passed through unchallenged and, veering a point north of the road, moving in the graceful slow-motion silence of a silver dream, faded into the desert. There was no pursuit.

Harry had in effect been concussed by the manipulation of his brain. He was recovering now, walling up the horror behind courses of anger, indignation, vengeful scheming and cruel anticipation. Such thoughts, he had long ago learned, as well as being pleasurable, suppressed to manageable levels the panic which rose like bile in his throat at any threat to himself. So he stoked his rage and indulged his morbid appetites, and while his blood ran hot his clever head ruled his timid heart and victories fell to him like corn to the hissing scythe:

Now, alone and unarmed, faced with a man who intended to kill him, survival would be victory enough. Harry pumped hard on the anger pedal. "May I rot in hell if I ever let you within half a day's ride of another woman of mine!"

Paul grinned. "It's not my fault if none of your companions wants to grow old with you."

"Is it true she's a mind-reader?"

"Yes."

"Gods! Is it true you are?" Paul shook his head. Harry, fledgling hope beating a tattoo inside his breast, tried not to register his relief visibly. "All right, let's talk practicalities. You can kill me, but probably not before I can make enough noise to bring here men who will despatch you, and without you I think those people in the desert will die also. Alternatively, I will keep vigil with you quietly until you are ready to go, and I will give you money and a written authority to get you past any of my soldiers who should challenge you, in return for my life."

"All right," Paul said negligently.

Harry laughed aloud. "No, I'm not that much of a fool, I shall require an earnest of good faith – else what's to stop you taking my money and my letter and then killing me?"

"What's to stop you giving me your money and your letter and then yelling blue murder?"

"You'd kill me," Harry said reasonably.

"You are so right."

"All right," frowned Harry. "Suppose I give you the money and the letter and you give me a dagger – purely for self-defence, of course?"

"I don't want your money, Harry," said Paul, "and I don't think any of your soldiers can read. And the only way you'll get a dagger of mine is between your ribs."

"Suppose," suggested Harry, his agile mind searching desperately for escape, "your friends are already in the hands of my men? With what shall you bargain for them, if I am dead?" When Paul did not answer he went on with growing confidence, "You saw them leaving, you know how many of my soldiers are outside the city. All it takes is for one to recognise Lockwood or the boy, or to think that Shah shouldn't be leaving with strangers instead of with me, and they are captives again. Maybe it has already happened and they are being held out on the road: my men must expect me to come soon, remember. If I don't —" He shrugged eloquently. "Anyway, there's no way you'll know until it's too late for you to do anything about it. You could walk into a trap. Unless you take me with you."

Paul snorted. "I'd as soon carry a snake in my bedroll." Yet a distance in his eyes suggested he was thinking about it.

"I won't give you any trouble," urged Harry, "you have my word —"

There was nothing wrong with Harry's argument. Had he ended it a sentence earlier it might have carried the day for him. But he was not psychic. There was no way he could have foreseen the effect on Paul that last promise would have. He knew nothing of the man's past or his particular ghosts, and when the thinking eyes went sharp and cold and frosted over Harry knew that he had almost won his life and now he had lost it, and he had no idea why.

Paul said only, "Your word is worth nothing," in a voice that cracked like the pack-ice.

The world turned perceptibly slower. Harry tried to shrink away but the bloody throne, hungry for another victim, held him captive. He struggled awkwardly to his feet as, flat-eyed, Paul closed with him, his slim blade disappearing between their bodies.

The voice in his head stopped Paul like a blow to the kidneys.

65

Clutching Harry to him, his stiletto already embarked on its journey from Harry's surcoat to his heart, the engineer spasmed as if electricuted and his hand jerked, momentarily out of control.

"Paul. No."

For a brief space the two men clung together as if engaged in some clumsy, sombre ritual or dance. Then Harry, sensing opportunity like a rope snaking through fog to a drowning man, not knowing the source of his deliverance but snatching for it with every fibre of his straining body, kicked and struggled with the galvanitic strength of desperation and tore himself free of the murderous embrace and in the scant hiatus before Paul regained command succeeded in interposing the carved back of the substantial timber throne between his person and the winking hungry knife.

Homicidal thoughts whirled in Paul's brain. "Get out of my head, woman," he gritted, pain beating in his temples. By effort of will he fought her out of his brain, but by the time he could return his attention to the assassination of the Barbarian earl she was there herself, in the doorway, an amorphous bundle of travelling furs and a calm gaze that transfixed him.

"Paul, no. I don't want you to kill him."

As he stood undecided, like an animal torn between training and instinct, the knife tight-clenched in his fist, the killing passion slowly passed, intelligence returning to the terrible blank eyes. He said gruffly, "What are you doing here? What's gone wrong?"

Shah shook her raven hair clear of her hood. "Nothing. I saw them safely on their way, then came back to wait with you."

"I don't need your help," he sneered, "or your company."

She came forward, closing the door behind her. "Or my opinions either, I dare say," she said coolly, "but you're going to get them for all that. I want Harry left alive."

"In God's name, why?"

"I don't want any regrets about this, Paul. I want to come with you and be with you and learn from you, and I don't want him getting in the way. I lived with him for three years. I shared his bed and his food and his campaigns. I never loved him. But if you kill him, his death will stand between us as the living man never

66

could. I don't want him haunting us. When I think of him, I want to picture him cheated and bitter and alone in his ice-palace in the north, not remember him coughing up his life on the point of your dagger."

"Then wait outside."

"Inside, outside: what difference does that make to *me*? Paul, *I don't want to feel him die.*"

Paul looked at her intently, as if concentration could recall his own lost perception. "Alive he'll come after us."

"I dare say you could slow him down."

Scowling, Paul turned his attention on the throne, small bits of Harry Jess showing between its carved spindles and crockets. "Quite apart from anything else," he growled, "the world would be a better place without the snivelling little dog."

Beneath his voice and his tone, Shah sensed a sudden lightening of Paul's spirit, a loosening of tension, and knew that – for better or worse – she had won Harry's life for him. Still, there was no need to tell Harry yet. She nodded ruefully. "This is hard to deny."

Harry, seeming to see his last ally slipping away, cried out to her in despair. "For gods' sake, Shah, you were my woman – you can't let him kill me!"

She shrugged. "I don't think I can stop him."

"You must. Shah! Listen, there are two of us. If you get inside his head, I'll take the knife away from him." Behind the throne Harry was practically hopping with anxiety. "I'll make it worth your while, Shah. I'll make you my queen: what do you say to that?"

"So it's to be King Harry and Queen Sharvarim-besh, is it?" mused the girl, laughter dancing in the eyes she turned on Paul. "What can you offer me to compare with that?"

"Nothing," he allowed. "Though perhaps I should mention he also tried to buy me off. Admittedly, not with marriage."

"If I believed him," Shah pursued mischievously, "I'd be sorely tempted."

"It's true," said Harry.

"However, having lived with the earl for three years I know him to be quite capable of lying, cheating, swindling, murdering and chucking his granny to the wolves at any moment it might suit him to do so, for his convenience or his amusement let alone his life. His promises are of approximately the value and enduring comfort of a spent match. I'll say this for you, Harry. At least you're consistently unreliable."

Harry stared at her aghast. His lips went on muttering, "It's true, it's true," long after utter hopelessness had filled his eyes. Quite slowly all the strength drained out of him and he sank on his knees behind the throne, his white cheek against unyielding oak.

"Hold him there," ordered Paul, leaving the room. Shah stayed where she stood, holding him.

Paul returned from the banqueting hall with the purple flask Harry had kept in the chest there and a syringe. "You told me Northlanders hadn't much experience of this stuff," he reminded Harry as he drew up the amethyst liquid. "Well, you're about to become the national expert."

They left the Barbarian crawling around on the throneroom floor, victim already to a maelstrom of conflicting sensations, not knowing if he had been drugged or poisoned. Aware of Shah's disapproval Paul grunted, "It was your idea to slow him down."

They found horses tethered untended outside an inn and liberated two of them. As they slipped through the west gate, the Ice Desert opening before them like an unfurled silver banner, Paul remarked, "Incidentally, if I find you inside my brain again, I'll blow your head off."

# Travellers

# Chapter One

Edmund's earliest recollection of the Ice Desert was of men with hawks: dark hawks, for the most part, with speckled silver breasts that flew on scimitar wings in pursuit of fat-bodied game birds flying south for the winter and north to breed. They were white when they passed over Chad, so that on a grey day they disappeared entirely against the pewter sky and the men did not know when to fly their hawks. But on a cloudless day the intense blue carapace above was the perfect foil for their plump snowy bodies and the hawks flashed like blades to the encouraging cries of their excited owners and struck the passing harvest out of the air with casual murderous blows of their talons.

Edmund's father led the hawking, an evil-eyed jer perched like a silver column on a black gauntlet. The jer, whose name was Beshaan, was so exquisite and so regally composed that people seeing her for the first time thought her a decoration rather than a working hawk. But the appearance of the first ptarm dispelled all illusions. The stately aloof jer suddenly sat up and took notice. Her great wicked eyes focused keenly on the sky and she flexed her shoulders and clenched her talons purposefully, and shook from her quills a soft, menacing rattle. Launched, her great white wings powered her upwards with a muscular grace that carried all eyes with her. She was a great white killing machine and the king loved her dearly and flew her on every possible occasion. She worked well for him, but everyone else avoided close personal contact with the bird. Edmund knew she had blinded one man and scarred just about everybody who worked in the mews. There was madness in her eyes. But she was a magnificent falcon.

Most of the nobles flew goshawks and a few of them peregrines. Jers were supposed to be a royal prerogative. No one took the taboo terribly seriously, but it was part of the tradition of a sport that was a rich tapestry of such injunctions and on the whole it was more fun to obey than disregard them. Similarly, a merlin was treated with a certain amount of disdain as a lady's hawk. Edmund, having first learned to fly a kestrel, had recently been promoted to a merlin, but the elegant little killer was too small to be effective against ptarm and so had been left behind, freeing its young handler to observe. Edmund was about nine years old at the time.

Perhaps that – having nothing to do but watch – and the novelty together were what made that earliest impression the most enduring. He had other memories of the Ice Desert – a caribou hunt, a journey to Leshkas; finally, most painful, still fragmentary and disturbing, the battle at the West Scarp – and some were more thrilling and most were more important, but for sheer visual impact none of them equalled that arcing of dark birds and white birds across the burning sky, and his father laughing as with wine as he flew the great silver death machine.

Nothing until this. And anyway the two things were different: the one a tableau, the other an ordeal. In the vivid memory of bright blue and brilliant white, of dark figures dancing tunelessly to an accompaniment of excited, unintelligible male cries, Edmund was a small boy watching. In this silver-grey limbo, so cold it bit, so featureless it seemed like to prove eternal, he was a participant: not even so much like one of the men as like one of the birds.

The great woolly camels paced tirelessly and without sound across the silver land. Edmund bestrode the cow Calipha, perched atop her load more like extra baggage than a rider. The bull Emir carried both Shah and Itzhak for long periods of time. Paul and Lockwood walked, silently for the most part, with as easy and effortless a stride as the camels. The calf brought up the rear of the little caravan. They were three days' walk west of Chad, except that Chad was not there any more.

Paul had turned away the horses when they made camp for the second night. Without keep or liquid water they could not subsist in the Ice Desert, and he said he lacked the facilities to butcher them when their reserves were exhausted. Edmund suspected rather that he lacked the inclination; which, in view of what happened the first day, was a paradox.

Edmund still had not got it straight in his mind. The facts were clear enough, but the enormity of it seemed to confound the senses; or perhaps it was the fever still lingering in his bloodstream that stopped him from seeing it whole.

After Shah turned back, to Itzhak's alarm and Lockwood's discomfort, the two men argued briefly whether to go on, go back or wait. Lockwood won and they went on, because the king's safety was of paramount importance, because it was what Shah herself wanted, and because Lockwood could beat up Itzhak with one hand tied behind his crooked back. All three were mounted then and they pushed on with as much speed as Itzhak, reluctant to leave Shah, could muster from the unfamiliar camels, reluctant to leave Paul. Lockwood, who had not even Itzhak's scant experience with the beasts, might have driven them faster but could not keep them straight.

Edmund was amazed at how quickly the Ice Desert closed in. On the brilliant days of the hawking and caribou hunts, the tundra glittered across long miles and a horseman could be seen when he was but a black dot on its pristine flank. But today, as if to aid them in their escape, the silver sky and the silver land met and merged and wove an opaque web around them so that the high walls of Chad grew blurry and amorphous and faded into the glimmering haze while the faint confused sounds of the exodus could still be heard within them.

Paul had given Shah his compass and Shah gave it to Itzhak. Itzhak had no idea what it was or how it worked, but he did know he had to keep the quivering arrow on the N and his camel's nose on the W.

After an hour Edmund, chancing to check behind, saw something dark undulating on their trail. The distance, the foreshortening and the ephemeral haze converted the horses' movement into something incomprehensible and quite alien. Itzhak would have urged the camels to greater efforts but now Lockwood called a halt: to greet Paul, if it was him, or meet the Northlanders, if it were them.

It was Paul and Shah on lathering black horses that snorted and snatched at their bits and smote the ground with ringing iron hooves. Paul waved aside Lockwood's relieved greeting. In a matter of seconds only he remounted his party – Shah behind Edmund, Lockwood and the poet on the Barbarian horses, himself taking the rein of the now much happier Emir – and, pausing only to recover his compass, led off once more at a steady, mile-eating lope.

Shah, clinging to Edmund's waist with determination, hoping vaguely that he too was clinging to something, thought this must be the closest thing to flight which men could aspire to, this smooth swaying pounding progress across the ice. The camel swung its long legs in lateral pairs while its bulky body swayed from side to side and its snake-like neck stretched out low and swinging to help its balance.

How long the wild flight continued she could not have said; but it ended at last, the beasts easing back into the purposeful, rugged walk, leaving Shah ennervated, trembling with exhaustion, her eyes blind with tears and her face fiery with cold. The horses slowed too. As he passed her Shah saw that Itzhak had his eyes tight closed.

Soon after that, rising land interrupted the icefield, black rocks frost-splintered, rimed with hoar, looming out of the haze. They altered course a point to follow their contour, Paul checking alternately his compass and horologram. He had not spoken for two hours. His face, when Shah glimpsed it, was dark and remote, uncommunicative. His eyes, narrowed against the wind, were cold and hard and swept through his band of followers almost without seeing them. Once in the headlong flight Shah felt Edmund's purchase on the swaying beast begin to waver and called for a moment's rest.

Paul reined briefly, took in the boy's condition at a glance and barked back, "I'm not stopping. If he can't ride I'll tie him on." Shah felt Edmund's wasted body stiffen with resentment. Dear God, she thought in despair, after Paul I'm the best rider here and I haven't been on a camel for three years. There's no chance we'll all be here when he finally stops.

But they were: Edmund more unconscious than awake, clinging to Calipha's harness with such tenacity they had difficulty breaking his grasp to lift him down; Itzhak wide-eyed, laughing and shaking all at once; Lockwood merely more dour and crooked than usual; and Shah so sore, and in such places, that much as she wanted to welcome the engineer into her bed and her body, she hoped it would not be tonight that the fancy took him.

Relieved as she was, Shah could not understand why they had stopped. It made no sense, to plunge recklessly across the hostile ice and then stop short with hours of daylight still remaining. There was no pursuit and though men and beasts alike, with the possible exception of Paul, were dead-beat they could have travelled further at a more reasonable pace.

Paul did not offer to explain. Their journey ended when he suddenly wheeled the bull camel into a narrow defile, a dark cleft where the flank of the mountain had suffered some ancient cataclysmic injury, and rode until the crowding rock faces leaned too close for continued progress. A narrow white ribbon far above her head was all Shah could see of the sky.

Paul slid to the ground before his camel settled down, folding on knees and stifles with gasping grunts in which could be detected a note of gratitude. With its head high on its curved neck and its hump decorated with pack and saddle, it looked like a rather ornate coffee-pot.

"We stay here tonight," said Paul. "See if there are any caves we can use. Lockwood, we'll need a fire: there are fuel rods in Calipha's pack." Shah watched him with concern and no understanding. Afterwards she told herself she should have known, but like Harry she had put it down to bluff.

The sound came like a rumbling in the mountain, like an earthquake, startling the camels to their feet and jerking snorts of fear from the timid horses. Inside the cave the five people froze over their Spartan meal as the dust of centuries was shaken from its roof into their stew.

"What the devil —?" began Lockwood; Paul waved him down, checking his horologram for the last time in the blood-orange light of the fire. "It's all right. We're safe here." He rose to his feet with an effort, no resilience left in him, and with a curiously flat expression moved to the cave mouth and into the defile. "Stay here."

Outside he pushed his reluctant body into a run, back the way they had come, to the bottom of the defile. He knew what he would see. It did not matter. He had to see it anyway. The bull camel watched him with lustrous eyes, unmoving, its great bulk primordial as the rocks.

Eastward across the Ice Desert the sky glowed rose and violet. A dome of flowers spread over the Garden City of Chad, invisible with distance, but above the flowers hung a great evil thunderhead, its roiling heart shot with storms, half as high as heaven.

Five hours. Many of them would have got out; perhaps most. Those who had the sense to travel into the wind and not turn back until the sunsets toned down in a week or two would survive – unless they froze or starved or killed one another in their panic or – What was the population of Chad? Lockwood said twenty thousand. Perhaps he had killed five thousand of them. Perhaps only two thousand. Oh dear God.

"Oh dear God, Paul, you did it. You really did it."

He started at her voice, low with shock and belated understanding, but did not turn round. "I told you to stay inside."

"What?" She stared at his back, fighting to keep control of her voice, struggling to command the rage and grief that welled within her threatening to burst her heart, failing. "You bastard, Paul," she cried bitterly, wanting to hit him, wanting to hurt him, wanting to make him cry (but if he did not scream he probably did not cry either), "you've killed twenty thousand people and you hoped we wouldn't *notice?*"

"Don't exaggerate," he said bleakly.

She gaped. "Well I'm sorry," she said then, nastily, hating him. "You think one or two may have survived? The prisoners in the city dungeons, perhaps, the odd hermit in the temple crypt? That makes all the difference in the world."

"I gave them time to get out."

"And somewhere to go to, Paul? Because without their homes and their stores they have no chance. Oh, the Barbarians, yes, they'll have leapt on their horses and been far away by now – like us. Except poor Harry. But the people of Chad, with no transport, no organisation, no reliable information – how can they survive? You've broken their city in a million pieces and scattered it down the wind. Between you, you and the desert, you've killed them all."

"Poor Harry?"

"At least he never knew what you'd done to him. But I know, Paul. I told you that dead he'd come between us. You gave me to understand you'd spare his life. Then you drugged him and left him helpless in an empty palace you'd fixed to blow up. Not one of your nobler actions, I feel."

"Poor Harry? Shah, have you forgotten what he was?"

"No. But I'm slowly learning what you are. At least his murder was on a human scale."

That one hurt. She had been probing for the sore spot, the place where he felt, trying to wrest from him some expression of remorse, of awe, of the terrible grief and guilt she felt and he must feel keener, and that was it. He jerked round as if stung, his dark face flushed, his eyes hollow with resentment.

"You think I don't care about those people? You're right. I can't afford to care. People always die in wars: too many people, innocent people, but I haven't so much blood in me I can bleed for all of them. Harry killed one lot getting into Chad, I killed another getting out. I could say I did it for the boy but it wouldn't be true because if it was going to work a bluff would have served as well as a genuine crisis. I could say I did it for you, but we both know that your freedom is a by-product. No. What I did at the pile was entirely selfish. It was my insurance policy. It was my guarantee that if I could neither talk my way out nor fight my way out I hadn't more than four or five hours in Harry Jess's hands to look forward to. I wasn't prepared to spend a week or more dying."

"You preferred to kill twenty thousand people?"

"Emphatically." The syllables he pronounced so precisely framed a bitter irony. "The death I gave them was kinder than any Harry would have allowed us. But even that isn't really the point. Survival is the ultimate instinct. It is most powerful in the most powerful and most pressing in the swiftest. To try and suppress it is counter-productive: when the fittest sacrifice themselves to the less capable evolution turns back upon itself. I have as much right to my life as any man in Chad: more, because I put myself in a position to safeguard it, which they did not. Furthermore, if I lose my life the world loses my skills, which are more important than any they command."

"One of you is more important than twenty thousand of them? My God, Paul, if it weren't for what you've done such towering arrogance would be laughable."

"Nevertheless, the world would miss me a damn sight more than it will miss all of Chad. What's one Ice Desert city, self-contained and secluded, more or less? There are plenty of others. With the king safe there may even be another Chad. That doesn't concern me. I was paid to do a job. By and large I've succeeded. What have I to regret?"

Shah, still staring, shook her head slowly, almost in wonder. Dusk had gathered while they talked, drifting like snow in the defile, piling deep and dense and shadowless among the rocks and dimming the plain, though the weak and fevered sun was yet proud of the horizon. The cloud had grown misshapen, heaps of leprous turbulence buffeting together where the crimson glow of fire now underpinned the destruction rainbow hanging over Chad. The perennial wind had developed a sick and fitful cast.

Shah said, "I'll give you this, Paul. You're the only man I've ever heard of who has personally turned the daytime dark."

Edmund did not believe; or rather, believing – for following on the events in Harry's throneroom the terrible dull explosion permitted no other explanation – and not accepting, could not persuade his heart of the truth that his brain and gut already knew, that if he were to back-track across the Ice Desert he would come not to the

Garden City but to the fragmentary ruin which took its place when the mushroom blossomed and the earth heaved.

The abiding weakness which had made the escape such a misery for him now came to his aid. Neither the shock, nor the grief – which was genuine, because he had many friends among those who had died – nor the almost hysterical feeling of indignation at losing his kingdom so soon after gaining his crown kept the lids from falling over eyes still wet nor the chin from dropping on the raging breast. With Lockwood's cloak thrown over him and Itzhak's fur hat under his head, twitching and mumbling in febrile dreams, he slept away the long and bitter night. None of his companions slept at all.

By morning the wind had risen. The omnipresent susurration had grown to the full-bodied eerie wail of a woman keening for a murdered lover, a tuneless dirge that scoured the nerves and threatened to repay murder with madness. The travellers swathed themselves in cloaks and furs, covering their faces up to the eyes. Cocooned in a chill limbo of howling wind and dancing ice-crystals that stole the horizon the little party, heads down, each alone with the grim thoughts they all shared, plodded resolutely westward in time with the swaying gait of the ponderous indefatigable camels.

An hour before nightfall the wind dropped a little, the note of its threnody falling from the insane to the merely deranged, and Paul called a halt. There was no shelter, they were far distant now from the mountains. Paul swiftly fabricated a small tent within whose rattling walls the travellers found relief from the soul-sapping monotony of ubiquitous, immutable ice. They were ice sick. It filled their eyes, gritty under the lids; its song filled their ears; its cold ran in their veins and in their brains, chilling physically and psychologically. The Ice Desert was a place not meant for men, and after two days their inaptness and inconsequentiality were like actual burdens weighing them down. Depression was the lot of those who ventured into the deep desert. Blue skies kept it at bay. The deliberate gaiety of a large intercity caravan disguised it. Familiarity eventually absorbed and transcended it. But for the mushroom shadow of Chad hanging over the low, wind-tom shelter

Paul would have been comfortable and at ease out there in the raging nowhere, but none of the rest of them would.

The trouble which Paul had to some extent anticipated began, unpredictably, with Itzhak. He was cooking supper over a rod-fired stove, and he looked up pensively and said to no one in particular, "With Harry Jess dead and Chad in ashes, the Barbarians will be away back to the Northlands. We too could go back."

No one answered, but there was no question that his remark had passed unnoticed. The king and the commander-in-chief of the vanished city seemed, without moving, to gravitate towards him by the intensity of their regard. Shah was watching Paul, covertly, as she had once watched Harry, waiting for the cat to jump. Recognition of that reversion to stereotype, even in that moment of restrained drama, struck her cold with shock: for if this relationship, of which she had had such high hopes, could degenerate so quickly into a mirror image of the other, perhaps it was unfair to blame Harry for his treatment of her. Perhaps there were natural victims as well as natural tyrants. The revelation, if such it were, paid her in humiliation and despair. Paul, meanwhile, was affecting uninterest in Itzhak's theory. He was sharpening the stiletto, the assassin's knife he now wore at his belt beside the slender darts; but the movement was not quite right, there was an uncharacteristic snatch to it; the activity was a blind.

Apparently unaware of the keen attention he had attracted Itzhak, still stirring, added with a silly grin: "Unless, that is, I was asleep when somebody explained where we were going through this white hell that was so much more desirable than a battered but presumably now quite safe Chad."

Paul polished faster, tight-lipped, until the knife flashed wicked gleams up at his drawn face. Lockwood left the stove and, even his bent back crouched beneath the low ridge, moved to squat beside him. "Paul, he's got a point."

"Lockwood, he's got a flat head."

All their conversations went like this now, the older man bitting his warhorse nature to stay reasonable and the younger making no concessions, responding when pressed with skilful cutting barbs of savage thrust but sometimes imperfect aim. Both were under stress: Lockwood's greater maturity and his experience of operating in a company of men gave him a discipline which Paul, who had never been anything but totally alone and whose intellectual brilliance and ruthless efficiency did nothing to mitigate his essential mistrust of other people, entirely lacked. He had never learned tolerance, which made him scornful of weakness in others and desperately afraid of it in himself.

Lockwood took a deep breath and said, "Not good enough."

Paul's hand stopped working. "What?"

"We're not sheep, Paul. We won't follow you blindly. There's no need for this secrecy. Tell us where we're going."

Paul eyed each of them in turn, taking his time, making them feel uncomfortable. He explained, as though to a backward child, "At the moment we're not going anywhere – we're fleeing. When it is safe to stop fleeing we shall start going to Leshkas."

He succeeded in startling them all.

"Fleeing —?"

"Safe —?"

"Leshkas —?"

"What in God's name is there in Leshkas?" demanded Lockwood. "Listen, if you don't know you should, there's a certain amount of rivalry between Leshkas and Chad, I don't know how welcome we'll be there."

"I know what there is in Leshkas," said Shah, her voice edged. "Another job for him. Another pile, another purse, another city, where he can stock up on the provisions he would have got in Chad if he'd left it standing long enough. Don't flatter yourself, my lord Lockwood, that our welfare concerns him. He won't permit us to interrupt the ordered running of his life."

Paul frowned at her, uncomprehending. He did not understand her anger when she obviously grasped the situation so well. "You don't want to stay here, do you? You have to go somewhere. Leshkas is as good a place as anywhere."

"Not as good as Chad." Edmund said stoutly.

"Not as good as Chad was," Paul corrected him. "Sonny, you're going to have to stop referring to the Garden City in the present tense."

"Thanks to you." There were no tears in Edmund's eyes but the discerning might have detected them in his voice.

Even Paul softened fractionally. "There will be a time when it's safe to go back to Chad, but it won't be for a while yet. I'll fix you up in Leshkas before I leave. Stay there. Grow up. Then go back and do what your ancestors did: raise Chad out of the tundra. You'll have more to start with than they had."

The boy's chin lifted. "And if I choose to believe Itzhak, that with Harry Jess gone I should return?"

"If you choose to believe a poet on the effects of a nuclear explosion you're a fool and deserve a fool's death, and if I weren't being paid to keep you alive I'd let you have it. As it is you're worth some valuable equipment to me, so I'll make you a deal. I won't advise you on iambic pentameters if you won't seek a nuclear education from a balladeer."

It was shortly after that that Paul went outside to release the horses.

A diplomatic minute later Shah followed. She found him carefully checking the horses' feet before sending them on their way. Paul registered her presence without looking at her. There was a new guardedness in his attitude that saddened but did not particularly surprise her. He was a man under siege, wary, entrenched, surrounded by unfriendly elements; she was sorry if he had seen her reaction as a particular betrayal.

She said, "Will they find their way back?"

"Probably."

"To what?"

"Why should I care?" he snarled. "They're only horses. I've killed anything up to twenty thousand people: what does it matter if a couple of horses survive or not?"

Shah sighed wearily. "Paul, love. What I think, what any of us thinks, is irrelevant. Chad is something between you and your conscience. It was your decision, now it's your burden and you'd better get used to carrying it. I don't know if what you did was justifiable. I don't think it matters now. Two things matter. Getting this little band of refugees to safety, which you won't do by antagonising them so much that they'll walk out on you and die on the tundra. And repairing this special thing of ours before it's lost to us and to the world. We have to get it together, Paul, on both counts."

"What I have to do is my job." He sounded stubborn but also faintly desperate. "This is my world, Shah. I know how to live in it. They don't. If they try to exercise their democratic right to individuality out here they're going to die. I can bring them safe through, but only on my terms, because those are the desert's terms. Why won't they trust me? Do they think I don't know what I'm doing? Or that I want them dead, so that I can chalk up a full house from Chad? Total genocide, is that what they think I'm after?"

"You make it hard for people to trust you. I know you better than anyone in the world and even I don't know when you're lying."

"Lying?"

"Paul, you lie like a trooper! You let me think Harry would be all right and then you killed him. You told me that there would be survivors in Chad: now you tell Edmund it still isn't safe to return. You wonder why we don't trust you? We wonder why you won't take us into your confidence. We're all on the same side, you know – we have to be. Don't force us into divisions we can't afford."

"If it comes to that, Shah, where do you stand?"

"Wrong question. If it comes to that you'll have failed, and the question is why."

He did not reply immediately. When he looked round the half-light found a kind of half-smile on his face. "All right, Shah, you've made your point. I never claimed to be easy to live with."

"Right enough," she agreed, "never you did."

"All the same, I hear no complaints from my camels."

"We're not camels!"

"Camels are more useful, more reliable and they don't talk back."

"Maybe." She grinned vividly. "But people are more rewarding."

Well yes, Paul thought, to the extent of a quatro-dimensional navigator; and he looked up guiltily as Shah touched his shoulder, afraid lest she had read the thought, but in her face he found no censure, only a kind of glow that he recognised with disbelief as affection.

# Chapter Two

He tried. At times Shah could feel him trying, as if it were a physical effort which brought beads of perspiration to his brow. She watched him sideways with baited breath and felt the restraint, and regret, as he let pass opportunities for his peculiarly cutting sarcasm. She had not realised that he derived pleasure from being rude. Slowly, as Paul's resolution held, Shah began to relax, the tension easing gradually as it began to seem they might complete their journey without further drama. But in her preoccupation with Paul's volatile nature she had forgotten that her other companions were also human, also under stress, and two of them were new to the business of taking orders. Even as Paul unbent, Edmund stiffened.

While they were on the move all was well. There was a course to be fixed and followed, camels to manage, sore places and stiff bones to ease and favour. Also, though the Ice Desert was bleak, it was not monotonous; not changeless, though most of its changes were subtle. A shading of the sky from silver through blush-pink to lilac; an interruption of the crazed ice floor where a petrified ice river rippled across its surface, corrugated like the bed of an ancient forgotten sea. Sometimes a mischievous eddying wind plucked at the ice and drew a haze of dancing crystals into the air, so that the camels appeared to wade, their spindly tireless limbs moving mechanically out of sight. Occasionally tall pillars of rock loomed out of the white, black and glinting with frost, towering inexplicably. In the far distance, when the light was right, the travellers could glimpse mountain ranges across their path, dark encampments like waiting armies.

But the main reason they did not argue on the move was the

wind. It had soon lost the sick confusion that followed the explosion, but even in normal times the wind was the most changeable aspect of the Ice Desert. It almost always blew, and always from the west, but within those limits all manner of variation was open to it. Sometimes it blew with a steady strength, without let or deviation, to a constant threnody of sound, for weeks on end, at which times those within city walls did not leave them and those without wrapped themselves in as tightly impervious a bundle of furs as they could devise, leaned into the gale, communicated with handsigns and practised swear-words in their aching, over-pressured heads. Sometimes it blew up into full-blooded storms, with lightning flashes bouncing between the livid roiling sky and the brilliant ice and thunder that rolled across the tundra like cavalry. In his solitary wanderings Paul enjoyed such dramatics; now he craved a smooth passage. Rarely the wind brought snow, in soft silent drifts or driving blizzards, and even Paul did not enjoy those: in the flayed open it was impossible to escape either tile extreme discomfort or the knowledge that it was conditions like these that finally got the better of the desert's most seasoned voyagers.

The danger point came when Paul called a rest halt, when sore and disgruntled people slid to the ground tired enough to be bad-tempered and not too tired to fight. Shah forestalled difficulties when she saw them coming. That she held a special position in the party had been recognised from the first. Perhaps it was her sex, and in grown men the shades of small boys doing as their mothers said. Perhaps it was the things she had in common with each of the men – with Paul her perception, with Itzhak her slavery, with Lockwood her caring, with Edmund her youth – so that, intuitively if not consciously, they saw her as a bridge linking their separate states. She did not care why they afforded her this almost diplomatic respect, only that they continued to do so, though it left her feeling buffer-bruised.

She and Edmund were watching the calf nurse. It spread its knobbly front legs and repeatedly shoved its Roman nose into Calipha's breast with such force that her front feet seemed momentarily to leave the ground. Her expression was that of a martyred Stoic. The spectators laughed, Shah a little ruefully. She had never had a child, which she supposed in view of all the opportunities meant she was barren, and all the days of her captivity this had seemed a blessing. With the promise of freedom, however, came the shadow of regret. Watching the great quiet cow with the faraway lustre in her eyes, Shah tried to make sense of her own rather woolly feelings. Some primitive envy was tugging at her like a hungry mouth.

Paul, feeding Emir from the meagre supply of concentrates, noticed the interest his beasts were attracting and thought it worthy of encouragement. "Thirsty?"

Smiling, Shah nodded at the calf. "Not as much as him."

"Her. It's a heifer-calf." He took a bowl from one of the packs and, elbowing aside the indignant and protesting baby, drew off a steaming pint from Calipha's capacious udder. The warm milk, rich and sweet, reminding Shah powerfully of home and childhood, filled her with a keen nostalgia. She drank deeply and with enjoyment before offering the bowl to Edmund.

Edmund declined, and seemed disappointed when Paul took the vessel without rancour and drained it himself. Paul gave no indication of having noticed, but Shah felt the shapeless turbulence in Edmund's mind that presaged trouble; and she thought that even without her special perception she would have been aware of the atmosphere, which meant Paul was trying very hard indeed.

Hasty in her effort to shore up his sapling tolerance she said, a little breathlessly, "I'd forgotten how good that is."

Edmund said, rather coldly, "Is that why you brought along a nursing female?"

"No," said Paul, "although it's a useful spin-off. I brought Calipha because I need her, and the calf because she also needs her. It's a good way for a youngster to learn desert-craft."

"And I suppose we can always eat it in an emergency."

Paul regarded him equivocally. "Only after we've finished eating you. That calf has a longer pedigree than you have, sonny, and would be a good deal harder to replace. She'll be the foundation cow for the definitive breed of Ice Desert camel." He looked up from the feeding calf and found Shah laughing at him and Edmund gone. He shrugged. "So you've discovered my secret vice: I breed camels on the sly."

She grinned. "Silly breeder."

Later Lockwood sidled up to her. "Is there any tactful way you can ask him to stop calling the king Sonny?"

Shah stared at him, sure he must be joking, but Lockwood scuffed sheepishly and nodded. "I know it sounds absurd, but it's getting to him. We have to be gentle with him, Shah. He's lost everything: his father, his city, his people, his self-respect. It doesn't make it any easier for him that he owes his life to the man who destroyed his state. He needs time to heal, and nothing chafing at the wounds."

Shah chewed her lip reflectively. "Listen," she said, deciding. "There's something I think he ought to know but I don't know if he can cope with knowing it now. Can I trust you to judge the right time?"

"What is it?"

"Do you know how the king died?"

Lockwood's face tightened. "By fire. The Barbarian made a point of telling us."

Shah shook her head. "He told you wrong. The king was dead before the flames touched him. He died quickly and cleanly by the grace of a man in the crowd who risked his own life to deal the king a kindly end."

After what seemed a long time, during which he stared into white space until his eyes burned, Lockwood blinked and sighed and murmured, "Thank God."

"My lord, it was Paul who killed him."

Understanding dawned in Lockwood's creased face. Other emotions also made fleeting appearances there but none endured. Finally he smiled. "Woman, I salute your wisdom and your courage. I shall hold this information until the king is strong enough to handle it. Then he will be as grateful as I am. But I think it's too soon yet for him to thank the man who killed his father." A frown wrinkled his seamed brow even more. "What a contradiction that man is. If Harry Jess had seen —"

"Yes. Time and again he risked his life for Edmund, his father, for us. Only at the last, when failure seemed all but inevitable, did he take steps to ensure that death would not be too protracted. He could have run then, my lord, and left the king to his fate, and in a few months no more would have remained of Chad than there is today. He too needs a chance to heal."

Lockwood laid his great ape's paw on her shoulder and smiled into her face. His eyes were compassionate. "Does he know you love him?"

Shah gave a quick birdlike shake of the head, eyes bird-bright with sudden unshed tears. "I shall hold that information until he's strong enough to handle it."

But the situation was too stressed, the personalities too volatile, for the quiet time to persist. If the journey had been shorter or easier, perhaps a strained peace might have lasted out to Leshkas. But as it was there was very little chance of the trek reaching completion without Paul and the young king coming to confrontation. The very vastness of the Ice Desert acted like prison walls, turning the travellers in upon themselves.

The conflagration came five days out and began with Paul plotting a new course, south of west, his all but featureless chart weighted to the ice by his compass, his slide-rule and his knees. Straightening up he remarked to Shah, "If we'd held this bearing much longer you could have met a colleague of yours."

"A colleague? I thought I was unique."

Paul grinned. "A predecessor, then. You know about Elaine? The last time I was out this way was when I took her back to her Order. She was on a recruiting drive when one of Harry's raiding parties took her from the caravan. I recovered her for them. It's a great barracks of a place, Oracle, like a little city, another thirty or forty miles on. We came in from the north that time, though, through the Jedda passes." He poked the chart with a fore-finger.

"I think you should ride over and pay her a call while we have supper," proposed Shah.

"It's a long way to ride to look at somebody's front gate," grunted Paul, "and that's all I'd see. They don't approve of men; no, not even that, they don't acknowledge the existence of an alternative sex. They had the greatest difficulty hiring me because none of them would see me or talk to me and they didn't want Elaine to either – notwithstanding the fact that she'd been Harry Jess's paramour for six months by then."

"It does seem to be taking modesty a shade far," admitted Shah. "Their virtue must be solid gold to need that much protection."

"I thought perhaps they considered me an unreasonable degree of temptation," murmured Paul, folding the map.

"You? Yes, well, possibly," agreed Shah, "as you say, they lead a sheltered life."

Lockwood was erecting the black tent with powerful, economic use of his great reach. After five days in the desert he had established a correct military routine for the making and striking of camps, during the execution of which even Paul kept out of his way.

Edmund, having helped unload the camels in a rather desultory fashion, had wandered a little distance from the encampment. Seeing Paul watching him Shah said quietly, "He's desperately unhappy."

As they watched Itzhak, his satchel under his arm, went trotting out to join him, his elongated body as ungainly in movement as a locust. Dark silhouettes against the great whiteness, their heads moved in a conversation which was dispersed by the wind before it reached the observers. Finally Itzhak threw up his delicate hands in a theatrical gesture of despair and stalked back, radiating umbrage.

Paul stopped him with a hand as he flounced past. "What's wrong?"

The poet was angry and upset. "He won't take his injection. He says he doesn't need it any more. He says —" Itzhak stopped abruptly, shuffling his feet.

"Yes?"

"That – that you want to keep him dependent on you. He said – hurtful things."

Shah slipped a comforting arm round his waist. He cast her a moist, grateful smile. Paul relieved him of the syringe. "I'll see to it."

"Make us something nice for supper," said Shah; as if it could be anything other than caribou stew.

Casually, a small dark figure easy in and somehow dominating his frigid environment, Paul strolled towards the unmoving youth. "Time for your trip."

Edmund's shoulders set frostily. "What?"

"The royal hypodermic awaits you."

Edmund turned and eyed the proffered instrument and Paul with equal dislike. "I'm taking no more of it. I told that fool Itzhak."

"That fool Itzhak cared for you like a mother when nobody else could stomach being near you. He also risked his life for you. Perhaps you don't remember."

"I remember being dragged like a dog in front of my father's murderer," flared the king, "and you and that pathetic idiot tripping over one another in your haste to lick his boots."

Paul, wondering if that were really the extent of the boy's understanding, shook his head, half bemused. "That doesn't matter. This does. Without it you'll start synthesising the stuff again and be back how I found you a fortnight ago." He offered the syringe again. "Will you do it or shall I?"

Edmund took the instrument and looked at it, amethyst against the light, and very calmly fountained the gem-bright liquid into the windy air. "I think not."

Paul breathed hard, remembered Shah's sermon and hung grimly on to his resolution. "In the interests of peace and good fellowship I shall look on that demonstration as a little youthful exuberance. Fortunately, there is more where that came from."

"You know where you can stick it."

"You're damn right I do," snapped Paul, "if I have to sit on your head while I do it."

Edmund fell back a pace and his voice dropped venomously. "Lay a finger on me and Lockwood will have your eyes."

"Sonny, I'm getting just a little tired of you."

Edmund, physically and mentally stressed as he certainly was, threw a tantrum to compare with Harry Jess's. "Don't call me sonny! I am a *king*!"

"Yeah," drawled Paul. "But not mine."

"If my father were alive —"

"He'd take you over his knee and spank you, which is what I shall do if I don't get some cooperation out of you bloody fast. In one degree or another you owe your life to every member of this party, but most of all you owe it to me. Well, that's all right, I'm being well paid; but if you ever become more trouble to me than a quatro-dimensional navigator is worth I shall dump you on your royal posterior in the middle of this desert and ride away without a backward look. It's just a matter of bookkeeping. I have no qualms about cutting my losses on an unprofitable contract."

"Which is doubtless," spat Edmund, "why you allowed my royal father to burn when anyone with an iota of courage could have saved him!"

It was not the challenge to his courage which carried away Paul's restraint. He had no illusions either about himself or the situation which had met him in Chad, and if he valued anyone's opinion it was certainly not that of a disturbed and bitter kingling. But nature had never equipped him for the role of philosopher. He responded with malicious honesty.

"Given a choice I should certainly have opted to save the king and let you dissolve in your own bad dreams. There was no choice. The abject failure of Chad to put up a defence guaranteed the throne a new occupant. But just for the record, it wasn't the Barbarian's torches that killed your father. It was me."

Another miscalculation: he did not know that Edmund had a weapon until the blade flared under his nose, an evil scimitar-shaped knife that the boy wrenched with a cry from his bulky enveloping clothes.

"Drop it," Paul murmured, knowing he would not, knowing that he had goaded the young king at least temporarily beyond the limits of sanity and not caring because he knew that armed with anything slower than a laser the distraught youth was his to take and wipe the floor with.

Edmund could not reply: words stuck in his throat. He did not know if it was the truth or a lie he was hearing, and in one way it hardly seemed to matter. It was a monstrous thing which raised new daemons in his tormented brain demanding the exorcism of revenge; so he lunged.

Lockwood, putting the finishing touches to his tent, looked up at the wordless cry carried to him on the wind. He saw the two figures, did not see the knife, saw Paul launch out two fast kicks to Edmund's wrist and chest that sent him sprawling. Lockwood was moving before he hit the ground. He passed Shah, and she, foreseeing trouble, took off in his wake, leaving Itzhak standing anxiously on one leg, wringing his hands.

It is doubtful if Lockwood made any attempt to weigh up the situation. He had no need to. For over half a century he had served the royal household; Edmund was the third king whose state and person had been his charge. He had worn the royal livery, carried royal arms and dipped his hands in royal blood. So unquestioning was his loyalty that the obscure provenance of individual quarrels were matters beyond his care or concern. He was a king's man and he loved the king, but even more than the king he held sacred the concept of loyal service. He would gladly have died for it, and would not hesitate to kill for it.

His opponent downed, Paul was backing off – he would never turn away from a potential assailant again. Lockwood, arriving like a small tornado, failed to appreciate that too: he saw the king on the ground, gasping, with Paul stood over him and intervened by the most direct means he could essay. He flung one long arm around Paul's chest from behind, pinning his left arm to his side, and locking his right wrist in the vice of his great hand wrenched his arm up and back to the shoulder.

Taken completely off his guard, expressions of surprise and the considerable discomfort of racked muscles startled from him, Paul lurched clumsily against Lockwood's barrel chest; and there the moment froze.

Shah, a little way back and a little to one side, saw each of the players in the tableau, saw what was coming and was almost fast enough to prevent it.

Lockwood, holding his man immobile from behind, saw only Paul and imagined he had ended the episode. Edmund swore

93

afterwards that, rising dizzy from his fall, with eyes still unfocused, he too saw only Paul, poised above him with his right hand raised in a manner only explicable if he had a weapon of his own. He surged to his feet, whirling his dagger two-handed, striking in fear and fury. The curved blade, razor sharp, slit the sleeve of Paul's padded coat with a whisper from cuff to elbow and laid open a corresponding length of the forearm exposed below.

Before the blood started, Shah gained control of Edmund's mind and petrified him; but it was already too late so with hardly a pause she released him, feeling as she withdrew the hysterical cocktail of horror and jubilation in his head. She was inclined to believe that it was not until then that he became aware of Lockwood, and Lockwood of him.

As they stared thunderstruck at the result of their unwitting collaboration, Paul said very calmly, "Lockwood, will you put me down now please?"

Lockwood gaped with wide, appalled eyes at the blood washing down over Paul's hand to pool a spreading stain on the hard ice. Finally he stamped the ground, violent with mortification, and stammered out, "Paul, I didn't – I never – I thought you – I couldn't see. I didn't know he had a knife! Edmund!"

"He struck me."

"Edmund, for God's sake! You stabbed a man while I held him. You have shamed us both."

A slow dark flush rose through the boy's cheeks. His eyes were stubborn. "I didn't know you were there." He was a king and a king's son and he did not apologise for anything; but beneath the proud disdain Shah felt a turbulence of dismay, shame, bitter anger and resentment running like a tide.

Paul was watching the pair of them quizzically, the king and the general, still locked in the moment of their disgrace; one eyebrow arched, blank-faced, his gold-flecked gaze sliding easily between them, he ignored the flowing blood that drew every other eye as with a magnet. At length his gaze settled on Lockwood. His voice was mellow, equivocal. "Do you want to do something useful?"

Lockwood nodded. There was pain in his face.

"Then make sure the king gets his medicine." He turned away, still with that dearth of expression. It could have been shock, for he was losing blood rapidly from the long wound, but Shah thought as she hastened to fashion a bandage from the hem of her shirt that it was rather a supercilious disdain for all of them and their human failings, as if he had long suspected that they were unworthy of his attention and this but confirmed it.

The gash was along the outside edge of his forearm, a little below the bone, neatly delineating the limit of his traveller's tan – evidence that he had been in a place where uncovered skin was not an invitation to frost-bite. It was nowhere very deep, but the blood flowed copiously.

"It's a good sign, really," said Itzhak, bustling up with his medical kit. "A couple of stitches, a dab of salve, a bit of bandage and you'll be as good as new."

"Don't write a sonnet about it," Paul said coldly, "do it."

Later, when they were alone, Shah – chin on chest, regarding him covertly – asked, "Does this change anything?"

Paul's eyes narrowed. His face was drawn and weariness seemed finally to have caught up with him. "In what way?"

She shrugged. "In any way."

"You mean, shall I leave a sick sixteen-year-old boy out here to die because of one more scar I was foolish enough to let him give me? Is that what you expect?"

"I don't know what to expect of you. Why did you tell him about his father?"

"It was the truth."

"And what," she asked with penetrating comprehension, "did truth ever do to you that you should derive such pleasure from barbing it?"

His eyes from under heavy lids held her in searching scrutiny. Finally he too shrugged, cautiously and lop-sidedly. "I enjoy the irony of wreaking havoc with honesty. Anyone can make trouble with lies."

Shah shook her head in despair. "And you wonder that I cannot anticipate you. It would take more than telepathy, Paul, it would take a crystal ball." She nodded at it. "Will your arm be all right?"

"It had better be. The closest thing to a hospital in these parts is Elaine's convent, and they only treat one another."

"Itzhak could probably put something on it, if you're not happy about it."

"Like badger offal, you mean? Skunk grease? An exotic salve of fermented bat and ptarm droppings? All Itzhak has in the way of desirable medical accoutrements are his hands; and if this goes sour on me nothing short of penicillin will do any good, and I don't think that's been invented yet."

Which extraordinary statement he was content to leave unembellished; or affected to be. Afterwards Shah was not certain if he had let slip the remark carelessly, a reflection of the currently low state of his mental and physical reserves, or if he had decided at last to initiate her into understanding of the greater mysteries. "Paul," she said, so profoundly mystified that her voice came out quite flat, "what in God's name do you mean by that?"

He answered by giving her a history lesson; and though everything he said was utterly strange to her, and much of it was frightening in that gut-level nameless way that things are which combine the alien with the familiar, yet the threads he wove formed a pattern too apposite to be dismissed as fantasy. It was inconceivable when the pieces of the jigsaw fitted so snugly that the picture might be distorted.

His eyes half hooded, somnolent and focused on the middle distance, leaning his back against a camel saddle, Paul began.

"There was once more knowledge in the world than there is today; also more people, and more cities, even in the north, and great roads that linked the cities so that a man could travel from one to the next in a day. The people then used their knowledge with wisdom and grace, to take care of one another, to prolong their lives, to give themselves comfort and pleasure, to seek after truth. They had the knowledge to make money, the money to buy time, the time to develop culture. The living was good and the people were one. This was in the golden days, after they grew out of pointing weapons at each other and before the plague.

"When the plague came everything was different. Everything the people had worked for and created now threatened them – their fine roads that made as nothing the distances between cities; the cities themselves, the throngs of the marketplace and thoroughfare, the great assembly halls and palaces of culture. They died in their millions, city after empty city reeking rotten to the sun.

"There were in that day scientists who knew the human body as intimately as I know a nuclear power plant, who established that the plague was spread by a micro-organism. They could find neither immunity nor antidote to it, but by identifying its method of contagion they were able to formulate a defence against what was by now a threat to human survival in all the lands of the world.

"Cities where there was no infection walled themselves up and refused to admit strangers. No one could come from a place where there was plague to one where there was not. The fine roads crumbled from lack of use: nobody travelled. Global culture ended. Cities turned in upon themselves, the city state was born. The end of communications sounded the death-knell for all the highest sciences: no one city had the manifold skills or resources necessary to maintain them. They had evolved beyond self-sufficiency, and they couldn't evolve back fast enough.

"The plague wasn't the only thing that killed people. Then more than now the prime power source for civilisation was nuclear, and when the plants needed the attentions of maintenance crews who were either dead or decimated the situation became critical. So did the power plants. Which is how my profession came to enjoy its singular privilege of free passage. Now that people move around more anyway there's nothing too special in that, but a hundred years ago, when the contagion was virulent, the nuclear engineer was the only point of contact between city states as insular as islands. He brought all the news a city ever received. He was the only messenger; he came only every couple of years, and even he was suspect – he travelled slowly between cities, alone in the wilderness for weeks at a time, so that if he had contracted the plague it would have incubated and shown itself by the time he reached his destination. God knows how many of my predecessors died that way, alone in the desert, turned away from the gates of the cities they spent their lives serving.

"The rigorous climate of the Ice Desert kept the contagion in closer check here than elsewhere. Here there were survivors of the plague cities, and refugees did not all succumb to disease although many froze or starved to death. From the ranks of the survivors grew bands of outlaws and brigands who gradually drifted together in the far north and were finally welded into a nation as such by Harry Jess.

"The world is become an archipelago, and most of the charts have been lost. Perhaps someone somewhere knows still how to prepare bacteriostatic antibiotics from the penicillium moulds; a surviving caucus of biochemists on the edge of the Dunes, maybe, or a new colony of thinkers evolving even now beside the Pewter Sea. But they too are islands – like the Oracle island and the place where I come from – and I cannot reach them, for we are not ships but driftwood."

# Chapter Three

The next morning the wind was up, new and old snow blowing together in crystal spirals that tore across the fore-shortened landscape. There was no sky that day and hardly any ice, just a modest circle of it with the little camp at its centre and the camels huddled down on knees and hocks on the leeward side.

The rising wind, howling its threnody to the bass accompaniment of the flogging canvas, impressed itself on the travellers even as they slept, and they awoke to the grey surge of the blizzard. Paul spent a short time assessing the force and direction of the wind before announcing that no useful progress would be made against it and the day would be better spent resting themselves and the animals.

It was a very small tent for five people to spend an entire day in. At first they relished the luxury of idleness. Back in the sleeping bags, over-tired bodies which had learned to rise and walk whether they felt so inclined or not now rediscovered ease and comfort and lazy hedonism. They stretched out and enjoyed the unaccustomed inaction, and welcomed the wailing wind as the bringer of good fortune; they talked in low desultory voices of nothing in particular, and from time to time they dozed. But even before midday the novelty was wearing off, weariness yielding to boredom and desert sickness to claustrophobia.

Itzhak returned to the subject of Chad like a man scratching a mosquito-bite. "I wish we could go back," he said wistfully, pillowing his narrow head on his hand and gazing at the ridge-pole as into space.

"But you know we can't," Shah appended hastily, hoping to turn the conversation from these dangerous straits.

"I suppose." But still the bite itched, and once again that alter ego which ran Itzhak into most of his tribulations gained the ascendancy. It showed in the unexpected challenge of his calm grey eyes. "Was it true, what you told the Barbarian?"

Paul shrugged. "I told him a lot of things, many of them lies."

"About Chad. Is it really gone?"

"That was not so much a lie as an exaggeration. Chad as you knew it is gone."

"But there is something left? – ruins, remains, something?"

"Yes."

"And survivors?"

"Oh yes. It's amazing what people can live through. They knew what was coming, there was time to get out. They would escape the falling masonry and if they stay away long enough they should also miss the fall-out. It won't have been massive, not like a bomb."

"And if they avoided the bricks and the fall-out, whatever that is which is not so bad from an exploding power-plant as from a bomb," said Itzhak coolly, "how shall they without houses or heat survive in the Ice Desert?"

"As we do." Hardness edged Paul's voice. "As the Barbarians do. The Northlanders have created an energetic and expanding culture with no more sophisticated power source than the strength of men and beasts and the fossil fuels they dig out of the ground."

"Chad is not the Northlands," Lockwood said, hunched over his knees and seeming to fill the tent. "Our people are city-dwellers, brought up in the sanctuary of strong walls. They know civic skills, and some of them know farming. None of them has any experience of a nomadic hunter's life."

"They'll learn. It's remarkable how radically you can change your life-style when your life depends on it. They'll move to the mountains where we spent the first night. There's game there. They'll find ways of trapping it. They'll survive. And in time they'll rebuild."

"I should be there leading them," Edmund said quietly. "I am their king. They need me; they have a right to expect me to be with them."

"Right now, Edmund, they need you like they need a hole in the head." Something strange had happened to the king and the engineer. Their attitudes had matured towards respect. "If you went back today they'd give you a messiah's welcome. They'd throw their arms in the air and shriek and yell and sing you songs, and you'd be quite sure you'd done the right thing. But you would find out that you had not. When they threw their arms in the air they threw away the snares and implements they had devised to tackle their harsh new life, that they would not need if you were bringing back the old one. When they rallied round you to sing and shout they were packing into a greater concentration than the tundra could possibly support. They would sit in a loving circle around you until they died. Scattered in small groups around the mountain they may all survive. Brought together in a poor apology for a court they could not provide enough to keep themselves, and in the end they would faction and fight for what there was and they would die unnecessarily."

"But that's not your reason for taking me away," the king suggested, watching closely.

"No," admitted Paul, "but it's none the less valid for that, and it's still a powerful argument why you should not go back until they can manage without you. As for me – my motives are purely mercenary. Someone you don't know values your royal house enough to pay me to conduct you to a place of greater safety until the situation out here stabilises."

"My father would have stayed."

"Perhaps. He would have been mistaken, but perhaps he would have stayed. But he would have made sure that you came with me. You cannot afford to hazard your life in that way, having not yet ensured your immortality."

"I shall return, when I am free to do so."

"I don't doubt it."

The wind blew like a mad thing, day and night, and then quite suddenly it had dropped and, striking camp hurriedly, they were on the move again. They made good progress, partly because they were strong from resting and partly because Paul insisted on keeping up a steady pace. He seemed to begrudge the time lost, as if he had to account for it somehow and was trying to make it up bit by bit. He never pushed them to exhaustion as he had that first wild day, but he never stopped pushing. When they stopped he ate mechanically, eyes on the horizon, or moved restlessly from one camel to the next checking their legs and feet and their eyes.

"We're damn near half-way to Leshkas," he grunted when Shah asked why. "That means we're as far from anywhere as we're going to be, and makes it a bad time for anything to go wrong with the camels. If one of them starts going lame I want to know about it."

"And their eyes?"

"Snow-blindness. They shouldn't be affected but it can happen. Then you have to smear their eyelids with a mixture of grease and ash."

"My," said Shah, fluttering her lashes admiringly, "the things a girl can learn from a man."

"Just remember," Paul said bleakly.

Oh damn you, she thought in her innermost self, do you suppose I forget anything you say – a word of your voice?

Over the next hours she noticed a curious thing. Each of the travellers was worried about Paul. One by one, discreetly, with studied nonchalance, they sought her out to tell her so.

Edmund was the first. He rode Calipha up beside Shah and slid from her back to walk with her. "We've covered some ground today."

Shah smiled at him. "Are you tired?"

"Me? No," he answered quickly; then slowly, wryly smiled. "Well, perhaps – in so far as us royals are allowed such vulgar failings. You?"

"Knackered," she said with feeling.

"What about him?" Like a god or a pernicious disease, there was a tendency to avoid saying Paul's name.

"You think he confides in me?"

"Is he all right, do you suppose? He's hardly said a word all day."

"In contrast to his usual non-stop flow of inconsequential

chit-chat, you mean?"

Edmund grinned. "I know, that constant bidding for popularity gets up my nose too. All the same, Shah —"

"I know. We're very dependent on him."

"It's not only that. If it's his arm —"

Shah linked her elbow through his in an unprecedented gesture of companionship. "That was an accident. I know it was an accident, Paul knows. He got no more than he deserved, he doesn't hold you responsible. Edmund" – she searched his face – "you do understand about your father?"

His gaze dropped. "Of course. It was a generous act, I don't know why I reacted as I did."

"Shock, mostly. Our beloved leader has when roused all the tact and delicacy of a rutting caribou. I should have told you myself, before."

"You knew?"

"I saw it. It wasn't an ugly thing, Edmund. It was a swift and dignified death for him, the thought of it need hold no horrors for you."

Edmund pressed her arm and could not speak.

Itzhak was next. "I don't much like the look of Paul."

"Never mind, perhaps you'll find someone more to your taste in Leshkas," said Shah.

He looked at her reproachfully. "I'm serious. I think he may be running a fever. It may be something or nothing but I'd like to take a look at his arm."

"So tell him."

"I daren't: there's nothing wrong with his other arm."

"What do you want me to do, hold him down?"

Finally Lockwood, purple with exasperation. "That damn fool of an engineer! He's dead on his feet: if he doesn't ease up soon he'll keel over, and where will that leave us?"

"Standing in a semi-circle round a hump in the ice, singing requiem and wondering how to divide two and a half camels between four of us?"

"It's not funny," Lockwood said severely. "If his arm is infected things could turn very nasty, for us but more especially for him. There's precious little in the way of medical facilities out here."

"No penicillin."

"What?" The soldier stared at her, angrily, understanding neither her words nor her manner.

"I'm sorry," Shah said, relenting. "I know you're worried. We all are. But there's nothing I or any of us can do. I don't know if his arm is troubling him, if he's ill or just out of patience with the lot of us. But one thing I am sure of: he knows what he's doing. He always does, Lockwood. When it comes to logic he's in a class of his own. It's ludicrous for amateurs like us to worry about him, and it would be palpable impertinence to offer our advice. If and when anything needs doing, he'll know what and he'll see that it's done. Paul sick? God help the distemper that takes him on!"

Cheered if perhaps not totally reassured, Lockwood grinned at her and shambled off, his powerful ungainly gait absorbing distance with the same casual disregard as the camels. Shah waited a little while and then quickened her pace slightly to join Paul without, she hoped, seeming to stalk him.

But her strategy was not subtle enough. Without looking up he grunted, "Edmund offered me his camel, Itzhak his medical expertise, and Lockwood an early death and a chilly grave if I don't immediately take to my bed with a good book or a bad woman. What can you offer to compare with that lot?"

"Well, I've no books," she said lightly.

"I have no luck," he said, and grinned.

"Seriously," said Shah. "How is your arm now?"

"It aches some."

"And you?"

"I've felt better. I expect I shall again."

"Itzhak thinks you've got a fever."

"Itzhak thinks I've got a doctor, and he's wrong about that too."

And that was where it rested until after camp was made that night. Languishing in the island of warmth created inside the tent by the little stove, idly watching Itzhak hover over the interminable stew as if this pot were in some way different, not boiled caribou but a blank canvas on which to paint unexpected culinary delights, Shah slowly became aware that Paul had been absent for rather longer than it habitually took him to feed and set the camels to rights. She listened and when she heard no sound of him moving about, mild interest yielded reluctantly to concern. With a martyred sigh she crawled over to the low fly and went outside.

They had come upon another outcrop of rock, an island eminence in the white wilderness, and to get out of the wind had pitched the tent in a deep fissure that reminded them all, too forcefully, of their first night out of Chad. The cleft was so narrow that the tent almost filled it; penned in, the camels had wandered a stone's throw into the rock and were contentedly chewing on their meagre rations, heads low and eyes somnolent. Paul was not with them.

Shrugging her furs around her Shah walked among the rocks. It was middle evening and the sun was still high – in that season it scarsely dipped below the horizon two hours either side of midnight – but nebulous, without strength. A pale pearl in a nacrous sky, it cast a gentle twilight glow over the winter world, compressing its hounds to a milky hemisphere no greater in radius than a man might stroll in a few minutes. Vet within this little world the air seemed preternaturally clear; the rocks loomed sharp-edged from the pale dusk, seeming to distill extra meaning from the strange light, a mystic waiting quality. There was among the rocks almost no wind.

Groping cautiously with her mind, Shah located the brooding consciousness that was Paul and turned her steps towards him. Flanking a group of large boulders she found him standing on the crest of a low ridge ahead, his rather small figure, less well protected than hers, silhouetted against the oyster sky. He was very still. After the initial moment in which she almost called his name, Shah found herself waiting too.

Paul's arms were folded over his chest and his head was tipped back, the dark hair stirring in the stronger airs above the rocks. He seemed to be looking at the sun. As Shah watched, uncomprehending, his head moved slowly back and forth against the pale heavens and she heard his voice, low and vicious and bitter with futility, murmur down between the boulders like slow lava. "Damn you," he was saying, "I didn't need this."

Shah did not understand, but the bleak despair in his voice filled her with a cold dread that spurred her up the intervening slope, his name on her lips. Startled, Paul swayed and his head jerked forward as he lurched round looking for her. Then she understood. His arms were not folded on his chest, the left cradled the right which was so swollen that the distortion showed through the cobbled-up sleeve of his jacket.

The face he turned to her was white and hollow-cheeked, undefended. His eyes, too bright and too deep in charcoal-dusted sockets, caught and held her in the mesh of his tattered emotions. Quite without resort to her singular perception Shah shared in his distress, felt the tumult in his breast of despair, disbelief, rebellion, rage and finally fear; felt his pain and the encroaching weakness which he could not stem, and the quick anger which had carried him through previous crises and could do him no possible service now.

Very gently Shah put her long arms round him and, lowering her head, touched her lips to the injured man's sleeve. "What can I do?"

She felt a ragged sigh escape him; he made no effort to break her embrace. He grew calm in the compass of her arms. "Firstly," he said, "don't tell the others we're in trouble."

"Oh Paul," she smiled, "they know. They've been plaguing me all day to do something about it."

"Damn. I hoped – how did they know?"

"They watch you like hawks. All their lives depend on you: that makes their interest personal. But not wholly selfish, either," she added reflectively, remembering Edmund's worried eyes, Itzhak's nervous hands, Lockwood's purple face.

"And you," demanded Paul. "Doesn't your life depend on me too?"

"Yes," she agreed, meeting his imperious gaze, "but I have an advantage over them in this. My life is not the most important thing to me."

"I can keep going tomorrow," said Paul, evading her declaration, "after that I don't know. I'll show you how to use the map. The vital thing is to keep them moving towards Leshkas. Don't let them turn back. We're more than half way there but it's against the wind; it would be quicker to go back to Chad but it would be a fast trip to nowhere. They would die, Shah – you must make them understand that. When I can't hold them they'll want to turn back, and you must stop them."

"Paul – Paul, slow down. What are you talking about, me and them? Where are you thinking of being?"

A tiny tremor ran through him like a chill zephyr. "Shah, I don't know. It's bad. I had my jacket off to get a proper look; I nearly passed out trying to get it on again. If it goes gangrenous —"

"Itzhak will put it right. You should have let him see to it before."

"No."

"He's really very clever, you know. Give him a pocketful of coloured potions and he'll fix anything from a broken leg to a childbed fever."

"Shah, this isn't a broken leg. It's infected. Poisoned. It's getting worse by the hour, and if it keeps on getting worse the bastard's going to kill me, there's nothing I can do about it. No, Shah, don't turn away, listen to me, please. It's important that you know what to do. If it goes black and stinking it's over. Out here there's no help, nothing to be done – you don't waste precious time bathing my fevered brow and telling one another I'll be better in the morning."

"For God's sake, Paul," Shah cried, "what are you saying?"

"That when I can't keep up any more you leave me. I mean it, Shah. If this doesn't get better of its own accord I'm dead whatever you do. I don't want you and all of them dead around me. That's what it would come to, you can't live in this wilderness for ever, it won't let you, and there's no point, no bloody point, no point at all —"

"Don't talk like that," she said angrily. "It won't happen. It won't. I'm not leaving you. It's not going to come to that."

Paul was not listening. A little choking laugh bubbled in his throat. "I should have known this job would go sour on me. It started bad and it got worse. The king, the boy – Harry Jess – Chad – Chad. Yes, well, maybe this is as good a place as any to call it a day. You can't follow a thing like that. Once you've destroyed an entire city state single-handed, dying is the only decent thing to do. After that anything else has to be anticlimax."

His voice, which had grown increasingly frail as he spoke, ran up like a reed on the last syllables. Shah felt his body go suddenly slack against her and he slid through her arms to the cold rocks.

Lockwood kept the late watch. It was not strictly necessary, but it was as well to watch the stove and listen for the camels, and to know if the weather was breaking up. Also, it was the only way any of the travellers could be alone, to stay wakeful while the others slept. Paradoxically, in this vast and lonely desert claustrophobia born of close contact with a few individuals in largely unchanging circumstances in a totally monotonous landscape was as real a problem as the cold and privation.

But there was little enough consolation for the keeper of the quiet vigil that night. The air in the dim tent, already thick with breathing, was also heavy with foreboding and fractured with tragedy. There was no peace in it, no solace, only a grey fog of almost tactile despair. There was no doubt in any of their minds of the gravity of the situation. Even as they slept their brows were furrowed with the knowledge, their fingers half-seen by stove-light twitching with the deep understanding that would not let them rest. The truth was too simple to be escaped: Paul's condition was critical, and if he died the others would probably not survive. Except the damned camels, Lockwood thought darkly, that would keep padding along through the worst of the weather until the smell of growing things brought them strolling out of the desert, with only their halters to show that once people had travelled with them but had proved less fitted than they to endure the northern wastes.

Roused from his gloomy contemplation by a movement too deliberate for a restive sleeper, he saw a crouching figure detach itself from the humpy carpet of sleeping-bags and resolve itself as Paul, his bulky bandaged arm strapped across his chest. They nodded to one another. Paul asked for Lockwood's knife. The soldier, wondering, slid it slowly from its sheath.

Paul took it without comment, felt the edge of the broad blade, then slipped it into the stove to rest among the little humming flames. Then he began to speak.

"I can't remember how often, in response to some small threatened iniquity, I've shot back with 'Over my dead body' – 'I'd die first'. I expect you have too. Well, I have news for you. We exaggerated. When it actually comes to it, when it stares you in the eyes and beckons, most things are preferable to death. That's the position we're in now, you and I; yes, the others too, because without wishing to brag I can't see any of you long surviving me, but we two in particular – me for obvious reasons and you because you are my choice.

"The irony of it is that where I come from a simple infection like this wouldn't cause a moment's anxiety. They'd clean it up, drain it out, pump it full of antibiotics and be very annoyed if it wasn't better inside forty-eight hours. You don't believe me. Hell, I don't blame you. Anyway, it's immaterial: I'm too far from home and too sick, and there are no antibiotics here.

"You're a general, you know about improvisation: it's the art of using what you've got instead of what you'd like to give you the result you want. What I have in my favour are you, that knife, this stove and the ice-cold. Under the terms of my improvisation you're the surgeon, that's your scalpel, the stove serves as a sterilising unit and the cold will, hopefully, both reduce the risk of further infection and improve my chances of not bleeding to death. I suggest we do it early, as soon as it's light."

Lockwood was staring at him, the hairs crawling on the back of his neck and up his forearms. "Do what?"

Paul smiled wearily. His face was terribly drawn but there was a kind of peace in it, a calm Lockwood had seen before in men who had suffered, who had the end in sight, and the end was bad and still they could cope and knew they could. It seemed to the soldier that nothing in life must be so bad that men could not triumph over it, if only in the dignity with which they yielded defeat; and nothing so bad that the circumstances could not arise in which it would come as a relief. He thought Paul was there now. After a long spell of weighty responsibility illness had obliged him to pass on the burden; the measures he contemplated were his only shield now against death, but death itself might kindly supervene. All of this was out of Paul's hands and so off his conscience; whatever happened he would endure because there was no alternative. There was consolation of a kind in that. He said, "Take the bugger off."

"Dear God, Paul," whispered Lockwood, "do you know what you're saying?"

"Lockwood, the bastard's killing me. It's not just that it hurts, it's the infection. If it's not gangrenous now it's going to be, and that doesn't get better. It creeps through you like a corrupt tide, killing by inches." He reached over and turned the knife in the fire. "I told Shah I could keep going tomorrow and so I can, but I'll be a lot sicker tomorrow night than I am now. My chances of surviving surgery are better now than they'll ever be: if you put it off too long there'll be no point. I told you, I want to live: I can take any amount of pain if I'm fighting a battle I can possibly win. I suggest you pick it apart at the elbow, it'll be easier than trying to cut through the bone."

Grief haunting his eyes, the memory of his own part in the tragedy rising in his throat like bile, all Lockwood could think of to say was, "Why me?"

Paul raised an eyebrow. Some of the tension had gone out of him now he had got Lockwood to accept the need for what he was proposing. "Who else? Itzhak may have more medical skill, but given a job like this he'd hesitate and I don't want anybody hesitating while I'm bleeding. Shah could do it, but it takes physical strength as well as courage to sever a limb and speed is important. The same applies to the boy, but there's a better reason for not asking him. In time he'll forget that he cost me my arm – it was, after all, more or less an accident. But he'd never escape the horror of hacking off the damn thing himself. Which leaves you."

"And am I immune to horror?"

"No. But you're not going to see anything you haven't seen before."

Shah said very softly behind him, "Paul, there has to be some other way."

Both men started. Paul's heart leapt within him like a startled animal, and the prospect of having to fight again the ground already won from Lockwood made him surly. "Do you suppose that if there was you'd think of it and I wouldn't?"

She touched his shoulder, edged up beside him. "Think what it is you're saying. You're an engineer, and you're talking of cutting off you right hand. What else have you tried? – I don't believe you've even let Itzhak see it."

"Damn you, woman, do you think I don't know I'm going to be a cripple for the rest of my life?"

"What about Itzhak?" interposed Lockwood. "He did a good job on Edmund."

"Itzhak did a good job of carrying out my instructions on Edmund. Look, I know you mean well, and I know that in your experience Itzhak is a skilled and knowledgeable healer. But where I come from his special skills are mere principles of first aid, and I've had more experience of first aid than most people."

"All right," said Shah, "I'll accept that. Then what about Elaine?"

"What *about* Elaine?"

"Who's Elaine?" asked Lockwood.

"You told me," pursued Shah, "that the women of Elaine's convent ran a hospital. Maybe they have some of this – penicillin. Let's go there."

"They wouldn't even see me."

"They'll bloody well see me! Listen, Paul, this is not just your problem. If you die we're all in deep, deep trouble. Even if you survive, it's going to be many days before you're fit to travel. I don't know if we can afford to stay out here that long. Have we enough supplies – for ourselves, for the camels? If you delay us much longer our only option may be to turn round and head back to Chad."

Shocked eyes flared in the dim light. Lockwood flinched from what seemed to him a cruelly selfish response. Paul recognised the deeper blackmail. "Shah, I *told* you —"

"I know. But if you're going to be sweating in a litter, caught between pain and drax, it's not going to be your decision, it's going to be ours. You think you're going to wake up tomorrow fit and well, only a little sore where the arm used to be? Grow up, Paul. You've lost control of the situation, and with one hand you're never going to snatch it back."

"What do you want of me?" he whispered in quiet anguish. "I didn't want this, but I can't ignore it. If I don't tackle it now it's going to kill me, and I don't want to die that way. Lockwood! You know it has to be done. Shah? You damn cowards, must I do the thing myself?" Before either of them guessed his purpose Paul had Lockwood's knife, its steel blade dull red from the fire.

Shah, who was nearer, grabbed his left wrist in both her hands, slowing his impetus yet knowing herself unequal to his feverish strength. "Help me!" she cried, waking the last remaining sleepers, and Lockwood swung.

With Paul crumpled senseless across her lap Shah carefully picked the roasting blade from his unresisting fingers. Lockwood looked at him with remorse. "I couldn't think what else to do," he mumbled.

Shah touched his hand briefly. "You did fine. Now we must act quickly, before he wakes."

Itzhak harnessed Emir while Edmund furnished a kind of litter from one of the panniers. Shah and Lockwood pored over map and compass. "The state he's in," Shah explained, "I have to travel. I don't know how fast that beast will go if I ask him, but I mean to find out. I should get there by mid-day; I'd expect you to arrive sometime the following morning. There's no point in you breaking your necks: once I get him there I'll only be sitting around waiting, maybe arguing some. I'll take the compass but leave you the map. Let Calipha follow Emir at her own pace; she won't lose his trail. Me? No, I won't get lost. Help me get him in the litter."

Lockwood lifted Paul in his arms like a child and carried him out to the waiting camel.

# Chapter Four

Though Shah never forgot that journey – for the rest of her life strange, trivial sensations and meaningless incidents would bring the images flooding back: a texture of wool like camel's wool, a bitter frosty night, a particular thready wind, and momentarily she was again on Emir's back, the steady rhythm of his trot sending the chiaroscuro desert pouring past her while the spangled sky wheeled slowly above – a surprisingly short period of time blunted the detail. Much later she found herself mistress of a small but classically formed regret that she could not relive the episode in all its terrible glory but from the comfortable rostrum of retrospection. At the time every frantic minute of it that she got behind her was another small victory.

It was colder than she had allowed for. With the coming of summer and the shortening of night, the sun rose in those days considerably earlier than the travellers. The worst cramps which held the few dark hours in a chilly vice had eased their grip before Shah habitually quit her sleeping-bag. Now the only radiance came from stellar pin-pricks light years away (Paul said: God knew what he meant) and there was no heat. The wind was an icy spear, thin, long and sharp, piercing her thickest clothes, lancing her flesh.

After an initial reluctance to leave his mate Emir was a tower of strength, a warm woolly machine of tireless piston limbs and economical energy. Twice he turned and had to be wheeled back onto his course; ever afterwards he held to the compass-bearing as if the lode were in his head, eating the night with long easy paces like a small constellation. Shah could not be sure if he sensed the urgency of his mission, but she had no doubt that he knew of his precious cargo and sought to make his steps soft on the jarring ice pan.

Bundled in furs, wedged in the leaping pannier, Paul tossed between semi-consciousness and total oblivion. Sometimes she heard him mumbling brokenly to himself; sometimes weak mewling moans as of an animal dying in a trap reached her, and then she sent out psychic feelers to the margins of his mind, soothing and reassuring like a hand on his brow, until he fell quiet. Once he cried out and the camel's ears semaphored a moment; then he dropped his head into the swing of his stride, powering along until Shah marvelled at his endurance.

She stopped briefly after the sun came up and burnt a fuel rod to provide water for the three of them. Emir took a small feed with his, Shah nibbled desultorily on a strip of caribou jerky, but she could get nothing into Paul but water. His skin was cold and clammy, and he received her ministrations like a drowsing man bothered by a fly. Once more she unfurled the fabric of their estate, to examine the threads as if she might find something new to confirm the wisdom of her decision. Yet she did not really doubt it. He had lost too much already: deprived of his last great talent she did not know what would become of him. He would make a graceless, bitter cripple; Shah thought she would sooner see him dead than destroyed to that degree. But she was a long way off giving up on him, and her resolve strengthened even as her physical resources ran down, like sands in a clock. She did not realise how exhausted she was until she came to mount up again and almost could not, standing panting against the woolly shoulder, betrayed by rebel muscles that shook with exertion, too tired even for tears. At the fourth attempt she dragged her aching body aboard Emir's apparently impervious one, and the camel surged to his feet and addressed his steps once more to the brightening day.

Back in the stove-lit tent, poring over map and compass, Shah had not doubted for a moment her ability to find the convent. There was after all nothing else out there. Now that very vacancy frightened her. Her objective was a mosquito-bump in the external wastes, a solitary heap of stones days from anywhere, in a wilderness where visibility was seldom good and sometimes non-existent. The compass would give her the general direction, but with no points of reference and no accurate measure of distance her chances of hitting the target were incalculably long. She was counting on her special perception, trusting that as she approached the little community its minds would be as a beacon to her. In the desert, where the only distraction was the proximity of the familiar sprawling mind now subdued and introvert with suffering, she had not doubted her ability to pick up the spreading ripples of mental activity. But suppose she could not – was too far off the line, too far away, too insensitive? Suppose she failed?

With the sun more than half way to its zenith Shah suddenly found herself grinning and for a moment could not think why. She was no less tired and only marginally less cold, and yet her chapped lips and wind-scoured face were creasing up in this idiot pantomime of delight. Then she realised why. Her subconscious, which was not dulled by bodily exhaustion, had recognised earlier than her conscious mind the advent within its field of new personae. Where there had been just Paul's frail, disordered emanation and the fuzzy imprecise – or perhaps imprecisely comprehended – emission which was how her mind educed that of the camel, now there was a new element, faint but substantial like the distant bellow of a crowd or the lights of a city beyond the horizon glowing in the sky. A murmur, a susurration, of thoughts like half-heard voices whispered to her like breath, and with gladness and relief swelling her heart she turned Emir's head through the few degrees that would bring them down on Oracle.

Like a little city, Paul had said, but she was not prepared for the vista of rose-red pinnacles and domes which lifted from the silver plain, impossibly high, impossibly pink, too exquisitely unlikely even for an hallucination. A desperate traveller, which she undoubtedly was, might have imagined a city wall, a way-post, a solitary well. Only a mad architect could have envisaged that glorious confection of towers, arches and spires stretching like petrified flowers towards the sun. A magnificent insanity reflecting itself narcissistically in its moat of ice, Oracle filled the traveller's eye from the moment it coalesced out of the morning vapours more than an hour's ride away. Bending over the pannier, Shah slipped an ungloved hand through the furs and cupped it against Paul's cold cheek.

"We've arrived," she said softly. "Don't you dare die now."

She rode around the wall, that towered sunset-hued eighty feet above her head, and it took her half an hour and confirmed what she had suspected from the first, that the only entrance to Oracle was a hanging bartizan at third-storey level, a crenelated gatehouse stepped out over a dramatic amount of nothing. Even the bartizan seemed at first glance to be pierced by no portal, although Shah realised that was impossible. Then, approaching, she saw and understood. The portal was a hole in the floor of the gatehouse, in which could be discerned the openwork of a large basket gently butting in its dock in the wind.

Shah's eyes travelled slowly down the featureless roseate wall and back again to the projecting winch-house. Then she shook her head, confounded. "I may get in there," she told the camel. "I may somehow get him in there. But frankly, Emir, I don't see any possibility of getting you in there."

Hard against the walls the view of soaring pinnacles and graceful upperworks disappeared and Oracle took on the uncompromising aspect of the fortress it undoubtedly was. Its rosy walls were solid and high and unbreached by any aperture below the level of the gatehouse. Above that level two flights of tiny windows nestled beneath a machicolation but there were no signs of life either at the windows or upon the wall or at the bartizan, Oracle might have been dead for a thousand years, or as many fewer as the winds of the Ice Desert would allow an untended edifice to stand.

Except that Shah could feel them within, feel the minds humming hive-busy behind the blank facade. Like bees, thought Shah, satisfied with the analogy, multitudinous and active but with a commonality of purpose not found in communities whose members were individuals before they were citizens.

Starting at the hanging gatehouse, using the projection techniques Paul had taught her, she explored outwards in concentric hemispheres, inspecting the minds she met until she was assured that at least a dozen of those within knew of her presence without, and at least half of them were watching her. She reined the camel beneath the nodding basket and raised her voice.

"I am Sharvarim-besh, I have travelled far, I am cold, tired and hungry and I seek your help. How may I enter your city?"

She waited. The silence sent clammy fingers creeping out from the walls, seeming to stifle even the wind in its campaign of stony indifference. Her probing mind felt a tiny shudder of anticipation beyond the wall, nothing more; as if the myriad minds of Oracle were as disciplined in their responses as the hands in their duties.

She tried again. "I know you're in there, and I know you know I'm out here. I wish to speak with the woman Elaine."

The hum of thinking surged again, more markedly. A high peak of activity somewhere in the group behind the gatehouse suggested to Shah that perhaps Elaine herself were standing listening there, but neither voice nor movement answered her call.

Growing prickly with irritation she threw back her furs. "If it's so long since any of you saw a man that you suspect me of being one, I am prepared to divest myself of this admittedly ambiguous attire until there is no doubt left in your minds. But if I do that you'd better get that rat-trap down here pretty damn fast, you'd better have something hot waiting for me inside, and it had better not be stew."

She got no further in her disrobement than the quilted jacket under her furs; then with a brief rattle and a whisper of winch the slatted lift began to descend.

It came to rest on the mirror ice beneath the bartizan, an oblong box about the size of the royal tub in the palace bathroom in Chad. Shah rode Emir up against it and slipped the straps which anchored the pannier at his flank so that it tipped its contents into the crate. "Don't you go wandering off," she enjoined the camel as she too slid from his back into the lift; then she shouted, "Haul away," and the curious conveyance swung free of the ground.

# Survivors

# Chapter One

A succession of wild thoughts crashed through Shah's mind as the crate pirouetted and lurched its way up the wall, the silliest and most persistent of which was that at some point someone would realise she was not alone and cut the cable. She expected to emerge in a room full of hefty young nuns sweating round a windlass.

No nuns, no windlass. When the cable drum finally wound to a halt Shah climbed slowly from the lift with mouth agape and eyes agog. The bartizan was furnished with metal cabinets that hummed and winked and whirred: there were buttons and numbered keys, though no one to press them, and spinning coils and chattering metal jaws gnashing busily away to themselves, and Shah had seen only one thing in her entire life which came from the same world as this and that was the Chad nuclear pile.

That raised more questions than it answered, but it told her one thing: that whatever Oracle was it was not a secluded order of unworldly nuns leading a tranquil existence of modest simplicity in the Ice Desert. With fear in her heart but also hope, because whoever they were instead of nuns they belonged to the knowledgeable portion of mankind that Paul had spoken of, Shah shrugged her coat and her courage about her and marched into Oracle.

She was ready for agument, even for violence. She was unarmed except by her special facility, which should prove enough but among people like this who could say? Were they really all women, or was that another well-cultivated deception? Shah came from a world in which people were men and women also ran; by trying hard she could visualise a scheme in which women were the sole authors of a desirable way of life, but her subconscious kept nudging in with the postulation: There must be a man behind it!

Which is perhaps why, in an effort to bolster her bravery, she pinned before her inward eye the image of Paul stalking into Harry Jess's throneroom as if he not only owned the place but had returned from a long vacation to find an under-gardener taking liberties with sceptre and orb.

The bartizan gave onto an awesomely long passage, dimly lit by the occasional high lancet, receding to either side into dark remote distance. The passage was of finely dressed sandstone, red like the curtain wall, plain but perfectly proportioned, and empty. Testing the ether Shah found the greatest concentration of minds directly in front of her, which was confusing as there was neither door nor archway. Arbitrarily she turned left, closing the heavy wooden door of the gatehouse quietly behind her.

She had hardly gone a dozen paces when a darkened aperture opened in the flanking wall, an arch of shadows framing a flight of stone steps. She could not see where they led, but they took her towards that concourse of minds and away from the sterile passage with its inhuman length and purity of line, which in its very emptiness made her feel exposed.

Inside the shadow the descending stair made a peculiarly graceful curve, sweeping down and round and opening with a sudden flourish of vaulting masonry, blood-red in the half light, into a cathedral.

The great chamber of Oracle was built – or carved, as from living rock – on the same Cyclopean scale as the mural passage and with the same fine appreciation of line and proportion as the sweeping stair. It rose, echoing silently, far above her head and fell away from her feet, an amphitheatre of soaring fans supporting an unseen dome, the figured tracery shooting into a darkness broken only and climactically by a lantern light in the very apex of the roof. Sunlight streaming in pale shafts down the still air, an oasis of calm in a windy desert, cast a pool of luminescence in the centre of the great sunken floor and caught in its spotlight, like ghosts frozen in a temporal trap, waiting figures, motionless, watching.

Shah too, motionless, a dark shape against the greater darkness, waited and watched.

They were all women: tall slender women of graceful mien in hooded dove-grey robes, standing in the centre of the chamber. They did not move or speak, or look at one another, and though all of them were facing in approximately her direction Shah could not be sure if they saw her or not; but they were aware of her. For some reason she hesitated to probe their awareness, collective or individual, deeper than that; and, at least for the moment, the need was removed when one of the women spoke.

"Sharvarim-besh, come down and be welcomed to Oracle."

At the foot of the stairs a gallery ran round the great chamber; at intervals around the gallery ramps gave access to the floor. Shah located the nearest and moved into the light.

The dove-grey hoods, turning imperceptibly, followed her as flowers follow the sun, with that same unforced uniformity. There was nothing regimental about their accord; it seemed more as if their responses were naturally identical, so while the apparently unconscious unison of their movements was disconcerting it was not in itself sinister; like a natural phenomenon threatening no danger.

The woman who had spoken before did so again. Looking at her Shah seemed to detect signs of authority or rank; not in her garb, which was indistinguishable from that of the others, nor in her demeanour, for they all shared the same bearing of aloof indifference. The deference showed in the grouping of the women. Each was perceptibly apart from all the others, but this woman was afforded a slightly but unmistakably greater zone of isolation by all her companions. She said, "You have made a remarkable journey. You must be fatigued. A meal is being prepared; come, accept our hospitality."

"Gladly," returned Shah, with gratitude but also with caution. She knew how much hinged on her handling of the next few minutes. "Not only for myself. My camel is also weary and in need of refreshment: is there a way it may be brought inside and attended to?"

"There is a place," the woman said obliquely. "The animal will be tended."

"Also," said Shah, taking her resolve in both hands and throwing back her head to look the taller woman in the eye, "I need your help for another. You have a hospital, people skilled in the repair of sickness and injury. I need advice, preferably assistance, hopefully supplies of – of – damn it, of a drug whose name I appear to have forgotten."

"You have a fellow-traveller? Where is this person now?"

"Still in the crate." The woman nodded, as if that explained something that had been bothering her. Shah hurried on, "We rode all night. Oracle was our only chance. It's a knife-wound that's become infected."

"Who is this person?" interrupted the woman.

Damn you, thought Shah desperately, you don't care who he is; the only thing you care to know you've already guessed. "His name is Paul. I owe him my liberty, as does another here. Oracle is the only place in this quadrant of the Ice Desert where he can be treated. You cannot turn him away."

The least whisper rippled through the gathering. The priestess, if such she was, enquired with studied calm, "You have brought a man here?"

Despair sparked Shah's temper. "You've nothing to fear from him," she snapped tartly, "he's dying."

"My dear, we do not fear men. We simply have no use for them."

"You had a use for this one when he was well. He risked his life for one of you. You owe it to him to care for him now."

"We owe nothing to anyone."

"Elaine does, and I doubt she's such an ingrate as to deny it. Is she here?"

"Elaine." The woman paused thoughtfully over the name, as if it savoured of something more than half forgotten. "There is no one of that name here."

"Of course there is, she's a high priestess," retorted Shah. "But she wasn't always a high priestess. For a time she enjoyed a less dignified role in Harry Jess's household; not to put too fine a point on it, a bed-role. Pardon my indelicacy, but you see I too held the interesting post of Barbarian's whore so I have little modesty left. I was relieved of my duties only days ago, by the same man who rescued Elaine from hers. This time he got hurt. He's in that bloody hanging basket now: in pain, fevered, only intermittently conscious, his arm badly swollen and possible gangrenous. If you don't help him he'll die. And if he dies I shall become extremely unpleasant to have around."

"Don't threaten us."

"I demand to see Elaine."

"Sharvarim-besh."

Shah was suddenly aware that each of the women was looking past her to the gallery; she was turning as the voice said her name. Another tall, slender woman was silhouetted pale grey against the dark stair.

"I am Miriam, High Priestess at Oracle. I was once Elaine; I am the one you seek. I have had Paul removed to the infirmary. Will you come there with me and tell me what happened?"

In the ensuing hours Shah came to know the one who had been Elaine and to enjoy her company. She admired her calm practicality, her unshakable dignity, and the rich and subtle shades of mentality and emotion which made up that attractive, intelligent persona. Shah also became acquainted with others of Oracle, but all seemed to lack the undercurrent of human warmth that gave depth to Miriam's character and conversation. If the difference was due to being bedded three times a week by a bad-tempered little Barbarian, Shah caught herself thinking, there was a case for making it compulsory.

Lost in the blind heart of Oracle, the infirmary was a complex of interconnecting structures at or below ground level. The main ward carried a low dome on short piers, received no natural light and was painted a paler shade of the dove-grey the women wore. It was empty.

"We hardly ever use it," said Miriam. "Since we have little contact with people from outside we don't get many epidemics, and nothing is more dismal than being sick on your own in a ward full of empty beds. We use the side rooms instead. It saves on heating, too."

"How do you heat Oracle?"

"Nuclear power, of course."

"How do you manage without bringing in an engineer?"

Miriam smiled. "We of Oracle built our power-plant. We need no advice on how to run it. But enough of our domestic arrangements. Here is your friend."

The little room was for all the world like Itzhak's cell in lost Chad, even to the colour and the domed ceiling. Inside, Shah realised, Oracle was all domes, all rounded feminine contours, swelling architecture reflecting female hips and breasts and swelling gravid bellies: an environment of wombs.

Paul without his clothes on she almost failed to recognise, which in view of her history was absurd. Quiet in the white bed, unconscious or sleeping, his head tipped to one side on the pillow, he seemed smaller than always, frail, the ribs too close under the skin of his bare chest rising to the shortened, stressed metre of his breathing. Drained of its colour his face had also lost much of its desert-beaten texture; translucent as porcelain his cheek held only a firey spot under the bone and his brow, the damp dark hair combed back from it, a heavy dew of sweat. His eyes were closed but for a thin white line under each, his pale lips parted sufficiently to allow a whisper of escaping breath. His left hand twitched mindlessly upon the sheet; his distorted right arm was sandbagged at his side. A fine tube ran an anonymous liquid into a catheter inside his elbow from a dripping inverted bottle above the bed.

Shah whispered, "Oh Paul," in a shattered voice and swayed.

Miriam steadied her and guided her into a chair. "I think you should be in bed too."

Shah shook her head. "Not while —"

"We'll do all we can for him," Miriam said gently. "He has a good chance here. You did well to bring him to us."

"I wasn't sure you'd help."

"Still you brought him."

Shah managed a grin. "I was going to play merry hell if you turned us away." A thought struck her. "Look, I don't know if this is a breach of your vows or anything – or if you'd be more comfortable if – well, I mean I can nurse him myself if you'd prefer, if you'll tell me what to do and give me what he needs."

Miriam laughed softly. "We have no fear of men, and we aren't made uncomfortable by them. It is simply that we find a single sex system more efficient than one of mixed sexes, so we take steps to perpetuate such a scheme of things. Those steps do not include watching someone die of blood-poisoning on our doorstep merely for being the wrong sex – even were it not that I personally owe a debt of gratitude to this particular man. No, we'll care for him, Sharvarim-besh – and you too, if you'll let us."

"I want to stay with him."

"Suppose we make up another bed in here?"

"Before you go," said Shah, holding out a hand. "I have another confession. Others of our party will follow us here. They too are —"

"Men?"

"All three of them. Well, more or less. The two camels are female," she added more hopefully.

Miriam smiled. "They can stay in the mews where we stabled your own beast."

"Paul's, in fact."

The priestess's eyes twinkled. "Not Emir by any chance? I must go down and say hello to him. I remember him with some affection. Well, both of them, actually."

The nurse made up the other bed – a proper off-the-floor bed like Paul's – but Shah did not use it, not until much later. She drew up a chair at Paul's left side and took his lax left hand in both of hers, and stayed like that almost without moving for the rest of the day and all that long night.

Two Oracle women were most closely engaged in the fight for Paul's life: the nurse who was in or near the room constantly and who monitored his condition by frequently consulting a battery of machines ranged behind the bedhead and occasionally looking at the patient, and a priestess who came to administer drugs and take away print-outs from the machines.

During one of her repeated visits to the little sickroom Miriam explained. "The machines trace all his vital signs and responses to treatment. Every hour they are fed into the diagnostic computer, which analyses them and prescribes accordingly."

"Penicillin?"

Miriam smiled. "I think we can do rather better than that."

Tears sprang to Shah's eyes all unbidden. It was not that she misunderstood. She appreciated what Miriam was saying, that Oracle had marvels to upstage magic and render the impossible commonplace, but the very word penicillin had become as a touchstone to her, holding concentrated in its slippery syllables Paul's best hopes multiplied by her own ignorant trust, more like a spell than a medicament. Losing it was like losing a point of contact with Paul, or losing something of him. She knew it was stupid. She was very tired.

He could not wait for her to grow stronger. His body a battleground for virile poisons and powerful drugs, his fever mounted towards crisis. Shah gripped his fingers tightly and fought his illness with an effort of will, cradling him in her mind until the spastic tremors eased.

Miriam, dropping by to tell Shah her friends had arrived, found her battling for Paul's survival with dogged determination, personal hatred of the thing consuming him, and virtually no reserves. As his temperature rose he had begun threshing and mumbling, gently at first but with increasing abandon. Twice his rolling dragged the drip feed out of his arm, sending droplets of solution and blood spattering across the floor. The second time the nurse wanted to tie him down, but Shah would not see him bound while she could hold him. So she held him: with her hands and her body and her mind touching the edges of his mind, finding turmoil and terror and anguish.

When Miriam finally managed to catch her attention she said, "What are you *doing?*"

Shah looked up briefly. She was not a pretty sight. Sweat plastered her hair to the brow above her sunk eyes, madly glinting coals in the pallor of her exhaustion. Her sleeves were pushed up above her elbows and her knuckles were white with effort. "He wants to die, he's got to get past me first," she said grimly.

# Chapter Two

Paul did not die. In what measure his survival was due to the medical science of Oracle, to Shah's determination to claw him back to life and to his own robust strength is incalculable, but certainly all those factors figured in his recovery. After interminable hours of having her heart scored by a sharp-taloned hope which outstripped conviction by several painful strides, when it seemed there was not remaining of Paul's life a big enough ember to be fanned back to flame, there was a quiet time and Shah yielded finally to sleep, her head pillowed on Paul's midriff, rising and falling gently.

The nurse, who found such unclinical intimacy distasteful, would have roused Shah and ushered her to her waiting bed, but Miriam smiled and signalled the nurse to leave them undisturbed. Paul's left hand had somehow wandered to Shah's jumbled hair and Shah was – very softly – snoring.

She awoke to the sound of her name, a whisper like an orphan zephyr wandered in off the plain. Deep weariness and a sleep fractured too soon had done little for Shah's mental processes, but she remembered the important things – where she was, why she was there and whose stomach her chin was making dents in – before she got her eyes unglued. Her heart leapt like a bird at her name on his lips; she drank his gaze, weak and hurt but intelligent at last. "Dear God," she murmured, her face aglow. "You're back."

His eyes slipped from her and slid across the room, superficially, without weight, taking little in. "Oracle?"

"Yes." Shah held his good hand. "They've been very kind. Elaine is here."

"My arm —"

"Does it hurt? It's getting better. You're getting better. We're going to be all right, Paul."

His lost eyes found her again. The flecks gleamed like golden fish in haunted pools. "My arm. I thought – I told Lockwood —" He could not go on.

"I know. It's all right." She raised his hand a little and bent her lips to it. "You're not going to lose your arm. You're going to get well."

He pulled his left hand from her gentle grasp and laid the forearm across his eyes. He drew a racking breath that shuddered the length of him. He mumbled, "I thought I was dying." He was crying.

Shah went to tell her companions the good news. It meant being lowered in the fretwork cradle, watching it return to its eyrie in the anachronistic bartizan, then waiting patiently outside the walls of Oracle until the miracle happened.

It was an electronic miracle, summoned by a switch, but when a whole section of blank rose-red masonry hissed loudly and raised itself higher into the air than a camel could stretch Shah could not contain a gasp of awe and admiration.

Behind the wall was a courtyard, inside the shelter of Oracle yet not breaching its defences. The moving curtain was only a facsimile of fortification: the real strong wall cut back behind the enclosure, holding the mews in isolation: invisible from the plain, without access to the city, it was a characteristically Oracular version of hospitality.

Still, Shah found the travellers established in some comfort in the quarters they had discovered there. Relief from the wind was itself a luxury, but the row of snug apartments, each dominated by a great hearth so spoiled the neo-nomads that they felt guilty about enjoying them. Opposite the apartments were stables, in which the little camel family was now reunited in approximately equal, if differently engineered, comfort.

Something strange had happened. She had been away from them – Itzhak, Lockwood and the king – barely two days. But so much had happened in that time that she now found she had grown away from them – even, in some ways, beyond them. It was not that she was less than glad to see them; it was not that they failed to share her joy. Edmund and Lockwood responded with giant grins, and Itzhak by weeping into an enormous violet silk handkerchief. They were still dear to her, each of them, because of what they had shared. But they were children. She had grown up. She had entered the tomorrow world of Paul and the Oracle women, and if time decreed she could not keep it nothing could rob her of its legacy of self-knowledge. Should she spend the rest of her life as a slave among barbarians, the memory of being among great intellects and accepted by them in a spirit approaching equality would remain a warmth and comfort to her. These were the days of her glory: she was one with eagles, and if fate should clip her wings she might walk with men again but her heart would cleave to the soaring wonder of flight.

When she went back to Paul's room she found him sleeping and Miriam waiting for her. Anxiety, too recently honed not to prick, stirred briefly under her skin but Miriam dismissed it with an impish smile. "Do you suppose he'll dissolve the moment you take your eyes off him?"

"Of course not," replied Sah, slightly nettled. "It's just a habit left over from the desert – looking after one another."

"No criticism was implied. He owes you his life."

"I owe him mine."

"And I mine. You're right – it does become a habit." They chuckled together like conspirators. Miriam went on, "Shah, can we talk? – not here, you might start shouting and Paul needs his sleep."

They went up on the roofs, entering an over-world of architectural surrealism. From the Ice Desert the filigree skyline presented a spectacle of bizarre beauty, its rosy filaments swooping and soaring with an airy grace that seemed to defy gravity. Here among the domes and pinnacles that illusion of weightlessness did not endure. The towering masonry was too solid, too massive, for fantasy. Instead, as the eye traced the monumental structures diminishing into perspective-points in the windy sky, the mind contemplated the awesome marvel of human achievement on this scale.

The wind soughed across the domes and wailed in the high spires; buttress arches wrung from it whole phrases of alien music. The two women clutched cloaks about themselves as they walked through the petrified landscape.

Miriam said, "Have you thought where you'll go from here?"

"Leshkas. Paul's taking the king there when he services their power-plant."

"And afterwards?"

Shah shrugged. "The next nuclear city, I suppose."

"Would I be right in assuming you want to go where Paul goes?"

Shah smiled faintly into her furs. "You would."

"Forgive me – has he said he'll take you?"

"You know him," said Shah, her chin lifting. "What do you think?"

"I never heard him speak of any companion other than his camel."

"Perhaps he's never known a telepath before."

Miriam looked round at her, startled. "You? Are you sure?"

"Of course I'm sure. I've been reading minds ever since I can remember. It's a less useful accomplishment than you might imagine, but Paul was once telepathic himself."

"How very curious," murmured Miriam. "And yet, perhaps I should have guessed. No matter. Indeed, all the more reason why —" She seemed to hear herself rambling and stopped, only adding a trifle abruptly, "There is an alternative for you."

"Really?"

"If he won't take you, or if you change your mind. You could stay here."

"Me – a nun?" Shah gave a positively lewd giggle. "I don't think I've either the vocation or the qualifications."

Miriam grinned. "You still don't understand about us. We are not a religious order. We are an island community whose purpose is to preserve and develop knowledge – every form of knowledge, medical, scientific, philosophical, social, aesthetic. Erudition is our forte. You cannot tell me that you have nothing to contribute, or

133

that you would gain nothing from concourse with minds such as are here."

"You can't build a life on intelligent conversation. Without wishing to be indelicate, I want a man. I want children."

"Many of us have children. I have three daughters."

Shah could not have been more taken aback if the roof beneath her had moved two feet to the left or a couple of its spires had begun to dance. Crazy thoughts lurched through her brain. She said cautiously, "Who – er – who is the father?"

"They don't have one. None of our children have fathers – only mothers. We do things differently here." Miriam smiled. "I'm sorry, this can't be making much sense to you. I will try to explain.

"A handful of the Oracle women have the same sort of family history as you and I: conceived by the sexual congress of a man and a woman. The majority came about in the same way as my daughters, by the artificial matching of cells from the mother's body alone. The process takes place in the laboratory. The neophyte is then returned to the womb to develop in the normal way. Because the children carry a full set of the mother's chromosomes they are perfect genetic copies of her: identical in chemistry, appearance, intelligence, aptitudes and all inheritable features. And of course, all are daughters."

"*Why?*" whispered Shah. It did not occur to her to doubt what she was hearing, though it went against learning as basic as speech and balance. Miriam's demeanour left no room for doubt.

"The development of cloning from a theoretical to a practical science was initially forced upon us by the same disaster that devasted all the world. Oracle was a plague city." High over the windy plain, her flogging clothes and still form silhouetted against the sky, the priestess spoke as if she remembered the desolate years. "We were a scientific research establishment, a self-contained township of men and women working contentedly remote from metropolitan pressures. We were physicists, biologists, chemists, and we enquired deeply into many mysteries.

"When the plague began, we of Oracle were ideally situated to contend with it, and soon we succeeded in distilling a vaccine.

134

There was no time for the usual exhaustive clinical trials, but with almost certain death as the alternative there was no moral dilemma. The plague's grip on Oracle was broken and it withdrew, leaving those who had not been vaccinated dead and those who had alive. We prepared to give the world deliverance. Then we discovered the fatal flaw in our elixir. Our vaccine, while slower and more subtle in its action, was even more efficient at depopulation than the plague. It caused total male sterility.

"The tragedy of it was overwhelming. We had fortified ourselves with the assurance that even if our partners and families in the cities were dead, if everyone in all the cities were dead, mankind need not die because we should survive and take among ourselves new partners, make new families. Now, though we might survive, our line was barren – if we were our race's last hope it would die with us. Unless the science of Oracle, which had betrayed us into this monstrous situation, could be made to resolve it.

"We began, naturally, by seeking a means to reverse the side effects of the vaccine. When it became obvious that none would be found, we turned our thoughts towards asexual procreation. It had been done before, with reptiles. The problem in applying the principles to people was that the human egg is very much smaller than that of an axolotl. Nevertheless, with all the specialised resources of Oracle concentrated on the programme, an answer was ultimately found. The clones inherited the earth; or at any event, this part of it.

"As it turned out, our worst fears were groundless. Oracle was not humanity's last chance. People had survived the plague; enough – being both men and women, and fertile – to safeguard the species. Oracle pursued no contact with them. We had always been isolated; now we were also alien – quite different, apart in every sense of the word. And – their existence underlined our loss."

Shah ventured an observation for the first time since Miriam's soliloquy began. "Your women could have borne children to men from outside."

"Indeed they could," agreed the priestess. "That was the danger, why Oracle finally closed in on itself, turned its back upon the world. For by then the advantages of cloning were becoming apparent. The bane of science is that, because of the years it takes to assimilate great knowledge, the best work is usually done by people approaching the end of their lives. When they die their discoveries may be preserved but their thought-patterns are not. But clones are genetic replicas of their parents. Their brains are structured on identical lines – they share the same approaches, the same appreciations. A clone can acquire from her parent much more learning than a sexually conceived child, and she is much more capable of developing the dead mother's theories.

"The advantages conferred on a community like Oracle by clone reproduction were so significant that the risks implicit in a heterosexual society were too great to be countenanced. Making babies with a man is more enjoyable than making them with a test-tube; so the temptation of male company had to be avoided. So began Oracle's tradition of celibacy. We have to persuade our daughters that men are undesirable, otherwise we might lose them and all the generations of achievement locked within them."

They had wandered beyond the forest of sculpted stone to the edge of the roof, and stood at the parapet looking out over the shimmering desert. From here, atop the landscape's only eminence, there was no relief for the eye until the glittering ice – pale pink, now, from some evening luminescence in the sky – merged with the horizon, and not much then. It was very beautiful and quite unyielding: a world on which men made no impact. A land fit for clones, Shah thought with a momentary twinge of bitterness she did not understand.

Miriam turned and flashed her a brilliant, tragic smile that startled Shah and plucked at her heart because she recognised it as Itzhak's, with all the implications that entailed. "I hope I'm not depressing you with this sorry tale. It's ancient history now, but it serves to explain what we are and why we live as we do. It should also explain why you would be particularly welcomed to our midst. If you are indeed telepathic, you have a remarkable gene to bring as dowry. And think of this: if you have daughters here, each will inherit that capacity. You couldn't be sure that any child sexually conceived would. Even if he wanted to, Paul cannot guarantee you what I can: a total communion of minds and spirits with daughters who will make rich your life and give you a kind of immortality afterwards."

There was a long pause. "It's almost," Shah said then, "an offer I can't refuse. If I were five years older, or two months younger, I should stay: I should grasp this opportunity with both hands and all gratitude. I am grateful, for the invitation. It's more reassuring than you know that someone believes I belong with them.

"But I am a freed hawk. I must follow the wind and my own nature, at least until I learn what each of them is for. Of the world I know nothing. I want it, Miriam, I want it all: I want Oracle *and* I want Paul and wherever it is he's going; but – forgive me – if I choose wrongly Oracle will still be here, but Paul will be gone.

"It may be that in afterdays I shall rue this as folly, learning that freedom is only another burden to shoulder and that unreflected love is a leaden gift that exhausts the donor and exasperates the recipient. It may be that by leaving I shall forfeit my best chance of having children: a concubine with nothing to show for three years' work is hardly a byword for fertility. If I find I have made a mistake I shall try to return, and cast my genes upon your mercy. At Oracle I know I could enjoy comfort, content, fulfilment. But I want something more. If I can possibly find it, Miriam, I want happiness, and for that I'm willing to turn my back on security and chance everything I have and could have to the frozen wastes not only of this land but also of that man. That's why, when Paul leaves here, I shall go with him."

"And that," murmured Miriam as they walked back towards the stairway, arms linked, "is exactly what I thought you'd say."

They parted outside Paul's room. Walking on, Miriam called back over her shoulder, "By the way, didn't you know? – Harry was sterile."

Itzhak's bombshell dropped soon after Miriam's. He arrived unheralded: there was a tap at Paul's door and when Shah opened it she found the poet standing on one leg on the threshold. She had dragged him inside out of sight before it occurred to her that the women must have admitted him in the first place and then conducted or directed him through the rabbit-warrens of the blind city.

Paul watched Itzhak's surprising arrival from on top of his bed, scowling irritably. Itzhak took it personally and quailed, but in fact Paul had been scowling irritably almost without let for a couple of days. He was impatient with illness, tired of restraint and inaction, grudging of wasted time. He thought he was fit to be up and around. Shah thought he should still be in bed. This was the compromise they had agreed, that he might dress and sit on top of his bed, but Paul had agreed with a bad grace and would now have welcomed an opportunity to be unpleasant.

"I – er – I've something to tell you," Itzhak began nervously, squeezing his hands together; "or rather, to explain; which is – oh, this is all very difficult! – why I'm not coming to Leshkas."

"Not coming?" exclaimed Shah. "Itzhak, of course you're coming."

"He's decided to become a nun," Paul hazarded nastily; and Shah felt a fractional guilty twinge because she had not told him of her own invitation to orders.

Itzhak smiled his gentlest smile, devoid of anger. "Not quite, but not so far away. I am going to stay here a little while. They're going to teach me something about medicine – what Paul would call real medicine. Then I'm going back to Chad." Forestalling the incredulous reaction he anticipated from their startled faces the poet hurried on: "They're going to need medical aid desperately, even at a quite modest level. I asked the women here if they would send a proper doctor but they said they had no dealings with the world outside Oracle. So I asked if they'd tell me what to do and they said they would. They're going to give me drugs and equipment and show me how to use them. I know it won't be like a real hospital, not like this, but I can set up some kind of clinic where they can bring their burns and their frostbite and their dysentery – and later, maybe their babies. I can be some help to them."

"You can die with them." Paul's tone was scathing but in his eyes Shah was surprised to discover concern. She bit back her own response. "You? You're worse equipped to survive out there than most of them. Getting you this far was a major test of ingenuity. How do you suppose you're going to get back to Chad alone?"

"The women said they'd help —"

"They'll help you get far enough from here that you can turn belly up without inconveniencing them. They don't care about you, Itzhak, and they don't care about the people of Chad. They don't care. You can freeze to death, starve to death, die of radiation sickness, choke on polluted water or have your head bashed in by some poor sod for a pair of good boots. You can go to hell on square wheels and take the whole damn world with you, and as long as Oracle remains untouched and the wind blows the stench the other way there won't be a tear shed here for you. Help you? These harpies wouldn't help bury you."

Shah said quietly, "That may all be true. But in view of what you owe them, Paul, you're not the best one to say it."

"What I owe them?" He rounded on her savagely. "Oh, you mean my life, my arm – little things like that? They did for me what you made them do, what they could not for shame refuse you. If I had come alone I'd have died out there on the ice, and only after they were quite sure I wasn't pretending would they have despatched someone with an ice-pick to shovel me out of sight."

Her voice dropped a tone and was chill. "The fact remains —"

"They're trying to buy you, Shah. Using me as the currency. They've asked you to stay, haven't they?" She nodded wary assent. "I know. When I was sweating on this bed and didn't know whether I'd live or die, Elaine came here. You were asleep. She whispered so as not to wake you. She said you'd be staying here. They want to get their hands on your perception. She said leaving you here was the price of my life. She was very reasonable about it. She pointed out that I had expected and received payment for my services to her, now Oracle expected a return for time and drugs expended on me. She asked me to promise I'd leave you behind."

Shah was scarcely breathing. Itzhak quietly took her hand in both of his. She managed, "What did you say?"

"What do you think I said? I was weak and in pain, and I knew damn well that if they stopped treating me I'd have to go through it all again, and I couldn't face that, Shah. I'd have agreed to anything they asked of me. For God's sake, woman, I destroyed Chad to save myself pain: do you think I'd baulk at telling lies?"

She had been backing away from him, a terrible trapped feeling beating inside her, betrayal stretching her eyes. She came up against Itzhak's long body and felt his hands clasp her shoulders, felt the unsuspected strength of him behind her, and through the mists of shock the memory of his enduring friendship and unfailing kindness gleamed steadfast as a beacon. Then the import of Paul's words filtered through to her. She mumbled uncertainly, "Lies?"

"Of course lies, what else? You don't seriously think I have any honour left?" He had come to his feet and stood swaying slightly, the spread fingers of his left hand touching the wall more for balance than support. "Listen. Soon now I shall be able to fight for what I want, and when we walk out of here no one will raise a finger to stop us. In the meantime I will lie, cheat and generally run the gamut of all the lower vices to protect our position. Yes, I'll bargain with you. I'll sell you outright if I have to. But God help the man or woman who tries to collect."

They stared at each other, as if meeting, across the tense and sudden silence. During the space the silence lasted Paul made an amazing discovery about himself: that another person – and by implication other people – mattered to him for more than just what he could get out of them.

Itzhak cleared his throat. "Well, I've told you my news. I appreciate the advice, but I haven't changed my mind. If I possibly can I'm going back. I'll go and tell Lockwood and the king now. Er —" he hovered a moment, smiling ruefully. "At the risk of making you laugh, Paul, I should warn you: if you let any harm come to her, you'll have me to deal with." He walked from the room with poise, and no one laughed.

Paul was left looking at Shah, and Shah at Paul.

"He cares about you," said Paul.

"He cares about everybody," said Shah.

"Funny thing," mused Paul, "I'm going to miss him."

"Does he stand any chance?"

"Maybe. Maybe I can think of something to stretch his chances. Shah —"

"What?"

"I didn't mean to frighten you."

"It's all right. I know where I stand now." I also know where you stand, she thought with a kind of shaky triumph. Just for a moment there, in the heat of the argument, you almost said you wanted me.

The thing Paul thought of to improve Itzhak's chances and to pay Oracle for his treatment almost broke him up. He told himself that soon he would have no further need of them, but they were not just the harvest of years' work, they were his friends. He gave Calipha to Itzhak and the calf to Miriam.

The poet was deeply moved by his gift, accepting it with tears in his voice and a lump in his throat. "I'll look after her," he promised, eyes limpid with gratitude.

"I know that," growled Paul. "The point of the exercise, however, is that she'll look after you."

His interview with Miriam was more difficult.

"I've talked to Shah. She wants to come with me."

The priestess eyed him calmly. "But you can't take her, can you?"

"Can't I?"

"You gave me your word."

"My word is worth nothing."

"And your life? Is that also worth nothing?"

"I can buy my life without selling hers."

"Then why did you agree to?"

"It's easy enough to blackmail a sick man. Harder to make him pay up when he's feeling better."

"You are, of course," observed Miriam, "grossly outnumbered. If we decide that Shah stays here, she will not leave. Paul, you know how long I have searched for a telepath! I was on the track of one when that damned Barbarian kidnapped me. I lost her; I'm not giving up on this one."

"It may not be that simple. You'd have to be sure of killing me, and Lockwood and Itzhak and the boy, and leaving her alive. Even then you'd only have her body, and it's not her body you're interested in, is it? I doubt she'd give you anything of her mind after that."

"That is why I would have her choose to stay. Though, in fact, we do not strictly need her consent. All we need are her cells and her womb. The next generation of telepaths will be of Oracle, and less independent."

"You're talking of —" he began, shouting, then stopped. His eyes slowly saucered. "No, you're not, are you?" he realised, shaken and impressed. "You're talking of clones."

"You're well educated for a technician," smiled Miriam.

"You've come a fair way for a concubine."

"Perhaps we are neither of us what we seem."

"This is true. Remember it."

Miriam frowned at him. "Don't force my hand, Paul. I don't want to see you hurt."

"At last we agree on something. Take what I'm offering, Elaine. I won't leave without her."

"I could – remove you."

"True. But you would hardly expect Shah to comply with your plans for her then."

"Compliance is not essential. She could be compelled."

"The word you're looking for is raped. Also true. But can you watch her twenty-four hours a day for nine months, until your cleverness bears fruit? Because you'd have to, or one way or another you'd lose her and her little clone."

Miriam elevated an eyebrow. "You really think she'd do that, Paul? Kill herself if she couldn't have you?"

"Me? Good God, no." The surprise seemed genuine. "I doubt she'd dampen a hanky on my account. But she won't be a slave again. She risked death to get away from Harry Jess: I don't think she'd be much keener to stay here, under duress. A little thing called freedom, Elaine? – do you remember it? Or don't you think back that far any more?"

"My name has been Miriam," Miriam said stiffly, "since I became High Priestess."

"And that's not all that's changed, is it?"

When the woman snapped to her feet, her fist ringing on the graceful sweep of laminate that served as a desk, shouting, "Damn you, Paul, I haven't been angry since I last saw you!" they both knew the worst of the argument was over. Miriam sat down again, slowly, smoothing the wrinkles in her habit and her composure. "So what are you offering me?"

Paul straightened up. "When Shah and I separate, I will make sure she has the means to get back here if she wants."

"And if she doesn't want?"

He shrugged. "Then you're out of luck."

The priestess sniffed. "It doesn't seem much return for all we've done for you."

"It's a gamble, certainly. If it pays off – and it might, she hasn't that many places to go – your reward will be rich enough. But in case she doesn't I propose sweetening the pot a little. Have you seen my calf?"

Miriam nodded, cagily.

"Take her. Clone her. She is the outcome of a long and careful breeding programme to produce the definitive tundra transport animal. In a couple of years she'll be the hottest property in the Ice Desert."

The priestess was openly amused. "Paul, we don't need pack camels! When we require transport, which we do seldom, we have something rather more sophisticated at our disposal."

"I guessed that," grunted Paul. "But none of the other desert cities has. Some of them have horses, most of them are dependent on caribou and their own feet. That calf's progeny will open up the desert for them. They'll trade for them with goods, treaties, alliances – anything you choose. If you want, my camels will join the cities in a network of new communications with Oracle sitting pretty at the crossroads."

"And if we don't want?"

"Power? Influence? You'll want."

"Perhaps." Miriam brushed the surface of her desk negligently with the backs of her fingers. "I dare say we shall find a use for your calf. Very well."

The desk shrilled. Miriam, frowning, fingered a contoured panel. A shutter rising in the opposite wall revealed an anxious, youthful face framed in grey and glimmering with cathode rays. "Lady – there are people outside —"

"What, our visitors?" She sighed. "Oh, you'd better let them in."

"No, lady," stammered the girl. "Other people. Men. Horses. They blacken the desert —"

Alarm deepening in her eyes, Miriam stabbed the panel again. More shutters rolled; the face disappeared. A bank of grey screens charted the flanking plain. From screen to screen stretched a waiting army, black horses standing snorting steam, black men with spears and studded clothes. They were thousands rather than hundreds, and they made no movement; a watching, waiting army.

Miriam, horrified, spun in her chair and stared at Paul. Her mouth was open but no sound came. Paul looked from her to the screens, studying the silent ranks intently, fierce-eyed. Then he straightened, looking at the startled woman over his shoulder, and the terrible wolfish grin grew and spread slowly across his dark features.

"Miriam," he said, finally getting it right, "I think we may all be outnumbered."

"Paul? Paul!" Shah's screech reached him through three intervening walls. *"Harry!"*

Paul threw open the door that gave access to Miriam's office from the long passage. "Himself? Did you feel him?"

"Paul, he's here – now – outside!" She lurched into the room a little behind her voice, her face flushed with excitement, dismay and something akin to happiness warring in her expression. She offered Paul no greeting: so adept a telepath was she become that she no longer equated meeting with visual confrontation. It was an unconscious slip from the norm of the kind which had marked her for what she was the first day he saw her. "Harry: he's alive!"

"And he's not alone." Paul pulled her by the hand and pointed her at the screens.

Shah caught her breath and sobered up abruptly. "Hell's teeth, didn't he leave *anybody* minding the store?"

Paul grinned savagely. "Be reasonable, girl. Would you come after you and me and Lockwood with anything less than the first team?"

Shah could not drag her eyes away from the black cordon choking off their escape. "He doesn't expect us to fight, does he?"

"He expects us to die." The tone was cynical, the eyes bitter. Between his eyes deep vertical lines betrayed the sick, furious frustration of impending defeat. He was loath to be beaten.

"Sod it," said Shah. It was amazing how empty she felt: empty of anger, empty of fear. "It's funny. When I felt around out there and found him, I was actually glad he'd made it. It didn't last long, though."

"It wouldn't," agreed Paul. He turned his back on the screens. He looked around the panelled room and his gaze fell on Miriam and stayed there until she broke the contact by shifting uneasily in her seat. His lip lifted slightly but it was hardly more than a sardonic smile. "Well, I suppose I'd better get down there and find out what he wants."

Shah wheeled and stared at him. "Paul, we know what he wants! If you go down there he'll get it."

The engineer shook his head briefly. "He wants more than me. There may be some room for manoeuvre."

"What room?" shouted Shah. All her sang froid was gone. "He wants us all dead. How do you make him change his mind?" She jerked her head back at the screens. "By force?"

"Hardly. Maybe some guile. Starting with you: you're the easiest one to disappear." He said to Miriam: "Get her one of your habits – you're about to acquire an extra nun after all."

"She'll be safe with us," Miriam said in a low voice.

Shah said, "No."

Paul ignored her. "Can you protect yourselves?"

"Oh yes," said Miriam with conviction.

"Paul, I said no." Shah's voice rang. "I won't watch you die from behind a veil."

"You're damn right you won't, you'll stay out of sight until they've gone, and if they come in here you'll use every wile at your disposal to keep away from Harry."

"They won't come in," said Miriam.

Shah stared at her, fresh wild hope kindling in her eyes. "You mean you can keep them out? Indefinitely? Then there's no problem. They can stay out there until they get tired and go away. Oracle could have been designed to withstand a siege: self-contained, self-supporting, walled, no doors. We could wait for the Last Trump here if need be." She was babbling to cover the silence surrounding her, and because the idea was not so extraordinary that it should need explaining in this way. There was another reason for the silence.

"I don't think," Paul said slowly, "there'll be enough habits to go round."

"Don't be silly," began Shah; then she understood. She glared bitter accusation at Miriam. "You mean, you'll protect me but not them?"

The priestess rose, stately behind her desk. Regret aged her classic face; the onus of responsibility weighed on her shoulders. "I am deeply sorry. But I will not risk Oracle, and that is what it would mean."

"If you can keep Harry away from me you can keep him away from them."

"I know Harry Jess. I think, rather than fight, he would leave without you, but he will not leave empty-handed. Yes, Oracle could repel the Barbarians. I could order a bombardment that would leave not a man on his horse; that would leave not a horse. And within weeks every city in the Ice Desert would somehow know that the crazy ladies of Oracle had a new terror weapon, and between wanting it for themselves and fear that we might use it against them every army on the plain would sooner or later line up out there and have to be destroyed." She jerked a hand at Paul.

"He only destroyed one state. You would have me destroy everything north of the tree-line. Four men's lives are not a good enough reason for a holocaust."

Disbelief and tears clouding her eyes, Shah stared mute rebellion. She felt fear now, all right, crawling clawing fear creeping from her belly to her heart up the inside of her spine.

Paul said only, "She's probably right," and made for the door.

With a wrenching cry Shah detached herself from the spot where she was rooted and threw herself on his arm, wild with distress. He stopped and stared into her streaked face, almost with puzzlement. He shook his head. He touched his fingers to her cheek. Then he swung, a fast back-hander that spilled her across the room. Insensible, she graced the floor like a dropped dress.

She was not unconscious as long as she should have been. Her urgent mind pressed the need for action on a reluctant brain still reeling from concussion, and her eyes were opening before she was capable of making a rational interpretation of the images they recorded; hence Miriam's unlikely stance half way up a wall. Shah sighed and the image wavered and slipped out of focus, and when it cleared she saw that what she had taken for the wall was in fact the floor, against which her right cheek was resting.

"Paul said I was to leave as soon as you woke up," said Miriam, straightening. "Please don't struggle, you won't be able to free yourself. I'll come back when they've gone." She closed the door behind her, leaving Shah alone.

Pain throbbed in her head and nausea crept up her stomach and along her throat. She tried to lift her head but could not without the use of her hands which were secured behind her back. Her ankles were also tied. Lying on her side, she tried to lever herself up on her elbow, but she lacked the strength; the strain on her stomach muscles only brought acid surging into her mouth. She coughed it out, wretchedly.

While she lay vomiting rancidly, the alert and urgent part of her mind stood somehow aloof, watching in despair and disgust and thinking, Damn him, even facing death he's still plotting, still dictating other people's actions. Had Miriam stayed she might have got into her mind, obtained her release that way. But Paul had told Miriam to leave when Shah awoke: he was not going to have her dashing up at the last moment for a death row reunion. He would sooner see her buried alive in Oracle, obediently churning out little mechanical clones. Shah had seen no future for herself as a nun, but she fancied the life of a glorified battery hen even less.

Groping unsteadily with her perception, which was as shaken as the rest of her, she found minds in the great hall below, but though she infiltrated one after another she could elicit no help from them: she felt their excitement, their apprehension and their anger but she was unable to make them respond to her. Her mental cries for help went unheeded.

She turned her concentration on her bonds, and on the nature of rope. She visualised the myriad fibres tightly twisted, each trapped by and trapping countless others, the integrity and strength of the whole assured by extreme inbuilt torsion. The key to weakening rope lay in untrammelling that twist, easing the pressure. She set her mind against it like fingernails picking at the shreds.

Itzhak did not know what was happening, but he was well aware that something was. He had been discussing surgical techniques with the priestess who had treated Paul. She went to fetch artery clamps from the next room and did not return. Minutes later a nurse put her white face through the door, saw him alone and patiently waiting, and scurried away, feet tapping a swift tattoo on the hard floor. It was the first sign of haste the poet had witnessed at Oracle.

Far away down echoing corridors and hollow halls, to the very limit of awareness in the voiceless, breath-abated city, he heard others: hurrying feet, running steps, a slammed door. He waited a minute longer, then set off to investigate.

Lockwood smelled the horses. The faint sweaty sweet miasma was so diluted by the crystal wind that it should have gone unnoticed in the secret enclave. But Lockwood had smelled it before, that curious heady mixture of animal power and dark angel grace, and that time he lost his army, his city and his king. Now the hairs pricked along his neck like a boar's hackles.

Edmund neither smelled the horses nor sensed the men, but he had known Lockwood long enough to recognise in the rigidity of his bent body and the set muscles of his face the emotion he thought he could disguise. Edmund, watching the old warrior with compassion – his flickering gaze, the perhaps unconscious posting of his sturdy misshapen body as a bulwark against the secret door – felt a most curious thing: a sudden lightening as of a weight he had been unaware of lifted from shoulders surprised by their own weariness. His voice was light.

"What, old friend, are we finally discovered?"

Lockwood's eyes bathed him, round with tragedy. "No," he lied thickly. "It's nothing. Stay away from the door. There is no one there. Only the wind."

Edmund smiled. "No wind ever turned you white, Lockwood; no, nor any Barbarian either, save that you had me to look after."

"The Barbarian is dead —" choked Lockwood.

"There is always a Barbarian. Still, I hope you're right: I would be happy to have outlived my father's murderer. Nobody lives forever – perhaps the best any of us can ask is to go after our enemies and before our friends."

"The city is strong," said Lockwood, talking too much and too fast. "They won't attack Oracle, and they can't stay out there for long with only what supplies they could carry. All we have to do is wait."

"They will attack Oracle," Edmund said calmly, "because they have come too far not to. And whether or not Oracle is strong enough to repel them doesn't matter, because these women will give us up to the Northlanders rather than risk their precious pink walls. And I, Lockwood," he added, finally managing to catch and hold the other man's eyes, "shall walk out to meet them before they start bargaining for me as for a beast or a sack of grain. I am the last king of Chad: I shalln't wait to be bartered by women."

"Paul," Lockwood hazarded wildly, "Paul will have some plan to deal with them. He always has a plan. He out-thought Harry Jess; he can deal with this mob. If you go out there now you'll waste all his work, everything he's done and been through."

"For once – and he may find it as difficult to accept as you do – there is nothing Paul can do. Those men have crossed half the desert for the simple pleasure of killing us. It won't make them rich and it won't make them famous, and when they've done it they'll have to turn round and ride all the way back again, and still they think it's worth it. How can anyone argue with motivation like that? It is vital to their military esteem that two men, a youth, a girl and a eunuch should not be seen to challenge the might of the Northlands and survive. Terror is their main weapon: they cannot afford to have it blunted. If we don't die, they'll be the laughing stock of the Ice Desert.

"Paul can't save us: he can't save himself. All the destruction of Chad bought was a taste of freedom for Itzhak, a taste of love for Shah, a lot of worry for you, a lot of pain for Paul, and for me the chance to face death like a king. It's not much to exchange for twenty thousand people, is it? – though perhaps none of them would willingly trade places with us."

He held out his hand. "Lockwood, I have treasured your friendship all my life, and the fates have provided that I may bear it with me to the grave if not beyond. I would not die in better company than this."

Too overcome for speech, Lockwood grasped the proffered hand, crushing the still slender fingers in his own bear's paws; then he dropped on one knee and pressed his weathered forehead to their joined hands. "My true king."

"My noble lord and friend," smiled Edmund, his heart swelling with the crazy contentment of a job well finished. "On your feet now, help me with the door. We have a last walk to take together. If God grants me grace this short while longer I shall not shame you again, nor shall any who sees this end of Chad doubt that it was a great city that raised a goodly people."

Harry Jess tugged the scarf away from his ruined face in an effort to focus his eyes on the solitary figure advancing across the ice. His eyes had not served him too well since the day when, his brain anarchic with drax, he had stumbled into the great hearth in the throneroom of the royal palace of Chad and lain in the stench of his own burning flesh until an opportunist looter, chancing upon him, decided there might be more value in a rescued warlord than a dented orb and pulled him out.

As the approaching figure grew, so too did the racing in Harry's veins. His heart hammered in his breast and his great horse, attuned to its master's excitement, quivered in sympathy despite the toll of the weary miles behind it and shook chaotic music from its jangling bit. The horse did not know what set its senses thus on edge, but Harry knew what galvanised his. Acuteness of vision is only one element in recognition. Harry recognised Paul before any of those with him made out his face. He pushed his agitated horse forward, halting only when his horse's champing head fretted above Paul's right shoulder, flecks of froth flying from its jaws.

Paul said by way of greeting, "I see you got out."

"No thanks to you."

"Indeed not, I hoped you'd burn."

Harry's voice shook with fury. "I damn well did."

Paul eyed him appraisingly. "Lightly toasted, perhaps. I had in mind a little pile of charcoal with a melted crown on top."

Harry's mailed fist clenched on the pommel of his sword; but the blade had hardly risen in the scabbard before he rammed it home again and hauled the black horse back apace. "No," he said then, half to himself. "You're not going to goad me into meeting you in single combat. I know my limitations: I'm in no fit state to fight."

"Which of us is? You remember that little prince I went to so much trouble to take from you?" Paul said humorously. "He stabbed me. I had to kill him."

"Oh, come on!" snorted the Barbarian derisively.

Paul shrugged. He pushed back the sleeve of his jacket, tore that of his shirt and picked the dressing away from the healing wound. It still looked suitably nasty.

"Well, well," Harry remarked after a moment. "Whatever made him do a thing like that?"

"I told him that I, not you, killed his father. It was no more than the truth, but honesty is not invariably the best policy."

Harry was beginning to grin. "But I watched the king die."

"You watched his carcass burn. I put a dart in his brain before the flames reached him. While everyone was watching my camel."

Harry's grin split his ravaged face. He shook his head admiringly. "You're incredible. Work for me."

"All right."

The Northlander laughed out loud. "So where is the prince?"

"Out there." Paul nodded beyond the horsemen. "I couldn't find the precise spot again."

"And Shah?"

"Inside. The women here will protect her. You've lost another concubine to this convent, Harry."

"Lockwood?"

"Also inside. They won't fight you for him, though."

"And – thingy?"

"Itzhak? Around somewhere."

"And the prince?"

"Dead."

"No."

Paul sighed and let his gaze wander away. "Harry, you're forgetting to be afraid of me."

Harry's grin which had been fading now vanished entirely and his eyes flashed hatred. "I was never afraid of you. I was conscious that destroying you could bring the desert states down on my head. But the situation has changed, Paul. Nobody values a nuclear engineer who blows up whole cities."

Paul's eyes came back, rising slowly over the horse and rider and finally fixing him, diamond hard. "What I did in Chad will be done to the Northlands unless you turn that horse around and get that rabble the hell out of my way, now."

For a moment fear pricked Harry Jess's scalp. It was not rational, it was instinctive. Then relief, the relief of a man wakening from nightmare, washed out the anxiety. "You can't threaten the Northlands. We aren't a nuclear domain. There isn't an atomic power-plant from Ragnarök to the Pack Ice. Anyone who wants to avenge you will have to do it my way, with horses and spears and bowmen. And he'll lose."

"You pigmy." Paul's voice was low, acid with disgust. "You don't even know enough to know when you should be scared. Every man with you" – he spoke past Harry to the waiting army, his words resounding now, magnified by the silence and the space, carried by the wind – "has friends and family in the Northlands. It's their home, and your power-base. If it is destroyed you lose everything. You go back to being a pack of nomadic bandits scavenging on the edge of civilisation. The first decent city you annoy will wipe you out.

"I can do that. Even dead. Those who avenge me will do it with a volley of detonations that will echo the length and breadth of the Northlands, every one of them dwarfing the Chad explosion. Together they will lay waste your land. If you are there when it happens you will die, all of you; and if you are elsewhere you will not be able to return within your lifetimes. Your province will be a toxic desert for the imaginable future."

For a shocked minute Harry almost believed him. He saw in his mind's eye the ravaged land, the blasted settlements, smelled again the noxious taint of burning flesh. He blanched. Then he managed a shaky laugh. "Hell's teeth, you lie good. But not even you can convince me you can blow up a battery of non-existent power stations in a province so far from anywhere else that it hasn't seen an invader in twenty generations. And even if you could, you won't – not after I've finished with you."

Paul's face was without expression. "You can kill me. But you can't get at those who sent me, and they'll bomb you to oblivion. They're not very pleased with you as things stand. They wanted Chad secure and stable under its own ruling family. They sent me to warn you off, Harry. I suppose it wasn't your fault I arrived too late to save the king, but they certainly blame you for the destruction of Chad, they'll be extremely peeved if you axe its last crowned head, and if on top of that they find you've taken unilateral action to permanently deprive them of my services, I give the Northlands about as much future as a roasted snowflake."

Harry was aware of a restlessness in the ranks behind him, an ominous muttering, and he was not sure who it was directed at. He said loudly, "Nobody can get at the Northlands. The whole essence of the place is that distance and the nature of the terrain between it and anywhere else make it impregnable. You couldn't take an army there – except an army of Northlanders. We know the ways and the pitfalls; we know where the food caches are, where to find fodder for the beasts. Without that knowledge I doubt your paymasters would get up the West Scarp; they certainly wouldn't get over the Tantalus. The glaciers will bury them deeper than I'll bury you."

"It won't take an army," said Paul. "The job will be done in an afternoon, by a handful of men, with weapons that fly at such unimaginable speeds that the whole of the Ice Desert lies within their range; and a great deal more besides. They will fly over the West Scarp, over the Tantalus, over the sulphur marshes, and cover the Northlands with a pox of explosions. A nuclear warhead is a much simpler device than a power-plant, Harry, much smaller and much more efficient in terms of destructive capability. You mount large numbers of them on missiles, point them at your enemy and press a button. Once launched the inter-continental ballistic missile is unstoppable; at least, it is now."

Harry Jess looked at him as if he were mad. "You're mad."

"Harry, it's time you recognised the fact that I know a lot more than you do. What I'm telling you isn't a figment of my imagination and it isn't a theory. It's history: it has already happened. Civilisations of a scale and complexity you couldn't even dream about have already been and gone, and some of the biggest of them disintegrated in nuclear confrontations. That was long ago, before the plague.

"We are of the Third Age. The First Age died with the bombs. The Second Age died with the plague. The power-plants are the last remnants of the old time; except for the men I work for. Alone of all the people on earth they maintain the nuclear deterrent. And once in a blue, blue moon they use it. I saw them use it once. I saw the results. I know they will use it again if you cross them. They won't bother to step over you. They'll flatten you."

"I know one thing you don't know," said Harry. "That girl you said was safe behind high walls has just come down in a sort of basket thing and is walking across the ice towards you."

Paul whipped round. "Shah? For God's sake, woman, go back!"

She never paused. Bundled up against the cold in the first cloak she had found, which was by the laws governing such things considerably larger than her own, she strode resolutely amid its flapping, a little like an avenging angel and a little like a line of washing. Harry remembered having her in his head and sweated cold. Paul thought of her lying trussed and safe in Miriam's office and snarled, "How did you get free?"

"I unmade the rope."

Paul, understanding, nodded slowly. "You're getting good at this, aren't you?"

"Harry —" she said.

The earl backed his horse hurried steps. "Stay away from me!" Panic wired his voice. "I'm prepared for you, witch-woman. Behind me there's an archer with an arrow in his bow. If I start acting strange he'll kill you."

"If my body dies while I am in you, Harry," Shah said, "I shall take you over."

The panic grew to terror and still the Barbarian held his ground. "You're bluffing."

"She's bluffing, I'm bluffing," said Paul. "You thought I was bluffing when I said Chad would blow up."

"You thought I would blow up with it." Slowly Harry's hurt reasserted itself, anger pressing even fear into some rear compartment of his mind. Like the rest of them, he had suffered too much to be thwarted now. He touched a gloved hand delicately to his spoiled face. "No, Paul, you're not talking your way out of this. I've followed you a long way and now I'm going to have you: you and her and the boy and Lockwood and the poet." Raising his voice enough to carry to the rank behind him, without shifting his eyes from the man and woman before him, he said bleakly, "Take them."

As the horses stirred forward a humming, grating sound came to disorder the military precision of their advance. The nearest riders clustered at Harry's flank, staring at the dark archway that had opened where before there had been the uninterrupted wall of Oracle. Two figures emerged, one slight and upright, the other low and massive. Harry grinned tightly. "Had to kill him, did you? Go on, Paul, tell me again how I must believe you because of Chad. Damn it, I bet you blew the place up yourself! Welcome, Your Majesty," he called. "I see the nomadic life agrees with you – agreed with you," he amended pointedly. "Well, four down, one to go – I expect he'll be along in a minute."

"I shouldn't be at all surprised," Paul muttered despairingly. He could not think what they were all doing. Sure enough, as they watched the lift was winched back up to the bartizan and reappeared a moment later bearing the unmistakable figure of Itzhak, long and thin as rope.

Paul made a last desperate attempt. "Listen, Harry. All this changes nothing. It's still between you and me. If I'm lying you can safely kill us all; if I'm not you'll bring about the destruction of the Northlands and everyone who lives there. That's what I'm talking about, Harry, total annihilation. Every bomb will flatten everything within half a day's march of the epicentre. Properly seeded the blasts will clap together like hands. There will be no pockets of lesser damage, no survivors. The firestorms will see to that. Those who don't burn will suffocate: the fires will suck up all the oxygen. For as long as the holocaust lasts there will be no breathable air in the Northlands. Every living thing will die. All your animals; all your wives; all your children, all your parents; all your friends. And if you go back, all of you."

"Cobblers," said Harry, with conviction. He signalled his men. The line of cavalry bent in a wide ring of muscle and steel.

Paul whirled round them, stamping in his frustration, still more exasperated than afraid. "Damn you, *why* won't you believe? Your really think you're invulnerable? I'm offering you a chance to save your race. Why don't you believe me? This maniac is going to write a death warrant for everybody you know and presumably care about. I can't put it plainer than that. How can I get through to you?"

"You can't," said Shah. She had been watching them – the blank faces, the tired eyes hooded against argument, the hunched shoulders of men wanting to finish their job and go home. "They don't know enough. Harry's clever enough to understand but he doesn't believe you. I can get through to him."

Paul eyed her with respect. "You unmade the rope, huh? I never heard that one before. I bet you – could —" His voice trailed off and his eyes sharpened, his gaze flickering from Shah to Harry and back. "Well now. There is a way out of this." Fastening Harry he went on, "I have to convince you, right? If you genuinely believe what I say you'll turn round and ride out of here because the alternative is unthinkable – apart from anything else, imagine what this lot'll do to you when you get north of the Tantalus and meet a smoking desolation."

Harry's lip curled. "You're playing for time."

"So you say. I can prove what I've told you is true. You can see for yourself. Shah will take you into her head and bring you into mine."

Three sorts of silence hit him. The dull, utterly uncomprehending silence of two thousand men whose minds could encompass nothing more sophisticated in the way of weaponry than the armour-piercing bodkin. A shocked and deeply apprehensive silence from those who understood the implications of that bizarre invitation. And from Shah herself an equivocal silence, speculative. Paul had an uncomfortable sense of her weighing up not only the feasibility of his proposal but also himself. Finally she said, "Is it possible?"

"Theoretically."

"You know what happened before when I went into your mind."

"This time we'll be better prepared. You've learnt a lot. You're much stronger, defter, more sensitive. And I'll be ready for you."

"This time there'll be three of us."

"Yeah."

"Like hell there will," snorted Harry. Alarm ringed his eyes, brought specks of high colour to his pale cheeks and injected a quaver into his voice. Harry felt to be rapidly losing control of the situation.

"You get no say in the matter." Paul hardly looked at him; all his attention was on Shah. "Even if you prefer not to know, your men won't let you disappoint them. After all, they have as much to lose as you, and finding out holds no perils for them – they can afford to be curious."

Edmund intervened. "Unless this is considerably less hazardous than it sounds, please proceed no further with it. If my death will suffice to end this bitter farce, so be it. I too am ready."

Paul disposed of the interruption shortly. "It would end nothing. If he kills me, my employers will destroy the Northlands; if he kills you and not me then I shall. You're only the prize, sonny, don't try to play the game."

"Nor," Shah said sharply, her chin lifting, "is it your decision."

For a moment Paul's eyes contested angrily with her; then he backed down. "No," he conceded in a low voice.

"All right," said Shah. "How do we do this thing?"

A soldier held Harry's horse for him to dismount; ostensibly a courtesy, it served equally to prevent the earl riding off in a panic. Chalk-white, with the lost eyes of a man who knew something but not all of what to expect, he joined the man and girl on the ice. There was a brief delay while Itzhak unsaddled Harry's horse and spread its blanket on the ground, then Paul and Harry and Shah sat down in the ring of horsemen, back to back, their shoulders touching, forming a triangle.

Shah said gently, "Close your eyes, Harry, and put your head back." She felt the tremor of his body, then the soft collision of his skull against hers. His hair, long and black like her own, had been worried into tangles by the desert wind. Shah wanted to stroke it, plant a kiss on his white and ruined cheek and coax the nervous rigor from his trembling body. She knew he wanted to kill her, but having him so much at her disposal, under constraint from his own men as well as his enemies, bewildered, frightened and about to be subjected to a monstrous assault, all made her want to mother him. Harry would have been glad to know it. He thought she was going to eat him alive.

Paul's eyes were closed too. Lockwood had seen them close and had seen, as lids still translucent from illness slid over night-orbs aureoled with gold, real deep fear. He had seen no fear there as he had throttled the man, long ago it seemed in the mews at Chad, none as they had watched Lockwood's knife grow red in the fire while Paul talked quietly of severing his arm. Lockwood wondered where the three of them were going that was more terrible than an al fresco amputation.

Shah went first. To the watchers she seemed only to slip into an easy doze, sitting cross-legged on the horse-blanket with her hands in her lap and her head resting against those of the two men. Harry yielded after a moment's resistance: a tiny spasm as captured muscles tried to obey the flight instinct, a small gasp of a sigh as that last autonomy was absorbed, and Harry went limp and only stayed upright because he leant against Shah.

Paul fastened his teeth in his lip and waited, blind face tipped to the sun, for them to come. When they came into his head he bit through his lip and the blood tricked slowly down his chin.

The first thing he did not understand, except that it looked like a fat arrow. It stood on its nock on more fletchings than an arrow would have, and its pile was pointed but not barbed. It was also much longer than an arrow: Harry did not know how he knew that. It stood on its nock-end in a shaft open to the sky and waited. Harry waited too.

The fat arrow caught fire. Flame belched between its vanes and billowed up its stocky flank, and the orange glare was such that all the detail was lost. The thing was no more than a scarlet silhouette in an orange firestorm. Harry's head – except that it was not Harry's head – rang with an unbelievable agony of noise, as featureless as the glare.

The arrow lifted. Slowly, in a manner entirely beyond Harry's comprehension, it raised itself up on a growing pedestal of flame, gaining speed as it gained height. A blazing comet of sound and fire, it curved away into the blue dome of the sky. There were no clouds.

The second thing Harry understood well enough. It was a city.

Not a walled city like Chad nor a loose association of settlements like the Northlands but something between the two – a packed nucleus spreading on every side in concentric waves of less and less dense occupation. It was vast, and somehow he was seeing it from above. Around the city, stretching into the dim distance, some of the land was green and some of it was brown. There was no ice. Harry was amazed: he had never seen anywhere with no ice.

The noise that hurt came out of the sky. It lanced Harry's ears and bruised his brain, and his eyes flickered patterns across the blue void as he sought the roaring arrow.

For a fleeting moment of atomic time he saw the thing. It was travelling almost too fast to be seen, plummetting from heaven towards the unsuspecting city, but he saw it because he chanced to be looking in the right direction when the explosion began. The detonation occurred high above the ground, triggered by altimeters which knew the precise height at which the death machine would wreak optimum havoc. Those who had sent it were a precise people.

When it exploded, of course, it disappeared. Everything did, in a flash of blinding light. Harry disappeared too.

He rediscovered himself some distance away. He could not see the city. What he could see was a giant roiling cloud, anvil-headed. The cloud was anchored to the ground by a thick turbulent column, its base fed by incredible fires, boiling smoke wreathing up the steam to be sucked into the immense cerebrum – being a Northlander, Harry had no experience of mushrooms. The brain-cloud was tainted by pewter and purple highlights that boiled away to nothing where the edges folded and flowed under. The air rumbled and moaned; sick sounds were wrung from the earth. God and his angels might have wept if they had not roasted in the first atomic bombing, which was some considerable time before this one, or moved away to a nicer neighbourhood immediately afterwards.

There was to Harry's eyes a certain Vulcan splendour about the explosion itself. All that sound, all that fury; the monstrous cloud devouring the land and feeding on the atmosphere; firestorms with all the sudden passion of summer thunder that swept and billowed and raised great seething pillars into the sky. But not even a Barbarian could have enjoyed the aftermath.

Harry wandered the shattered city like a ghost. It was not completely flattened. Here and there a building sturdier than others had left a comer projecting stories high from the devastation, accusing fingers stabbing at the sky whence the terror had come. The sky was no longer blue. It was grey and khaki, shot with livid belts of violet and magenta, and it was low. There was no sun. A shade lay over the land.

The fingers of masonry, like ruined towers or gantries, rose from a rubble plain. The rubble was flashed and charred, and quite unidentifiable. There was nothing to say what it had been: houses or public buildings or bridges or stores or stables. Now the stones had gone to glass and the glass had melted they were all the same. The whole city was become a vitreous quarry. Of course, there had been things other than stone and glass in the city, but they had not survived even to the meagre extent of adding to the rubble. The organic things and the soft inorganic things had vaporised and the metals had run like water. The metals were there still, congealed in hidden pools beneath the boulders, but here under the epicentre of the blast there were no bodies, not even charred ones, not even ones gone to ash. The cataclysm had been so total that not only were there no living people left, there were no dead ones either.

Harry travelled away from the heart of the city. The desolation stretched beyond where the city yielded to suburn and beyond where the suburbs yielded to a succession of loosely associated satellite villages that reminded him uncomfortably of home. The degree of devastation moderated with distance, but he had gone a long way before he saw the first bodies. Even then he did not know what they were. They were amorphous, carbonised, ashy hummocks: only when he came on one which freak chance had partially shielded and saw bare legs, hardly scorched, attached to a shapeless grey bundle like the other shapeless grey bundles did he realise that the countless people who had lived here and died here were here still: that the tortured landscape was a crematorium.

Further on the bodies were more recognisably bodies. The diminishing force of the blast had spared them vestiges of personality:

size, sex, fragments of clothing, melted rings on burnt fingers. Some even had faces. He saw one woman hung on a railing whose front was sufficiently undamaged that he could see the expression on her face and whose back was charred to the skeleton. Her expression was one of surprise.

Yet worse than the dead were the living, when he finally found them. People sporting the most terrible burns and injuries wandered round in a daze, aimlessly, too shocked even to fall down. None of them cried; not the children, not the women. There was no one to cry to: they were all in the same state. Concentric rings of bodily hurt had replaced those of civic structure which existed before the arrow, before the cloud. The geography of the shattered place was echoed in isobars of human ruin.

And Harry knew, without knowing how he knew, that none of these people would long survive the lost masses of the inner city; that they would all die, soon, and that what would kill them would be not their burns, their flayed skins, or even their blasted sterile world, but something more insidiously murderous – something stalking them silent and unseen, seeping into them unnoticed, an irresistible creeping destruction that had them all fingered. He thought it had something to do with the cloud.

"Thank God," a voice said behind him, flat with exhausted passion, hoarse with screaming done. "Thank God you've come." It was the first human sound Harry had heard in this ruined place, and at it he lurched round as if seared.

It was a woman. She might have been young before the bomb; it was hard to tell. She was dressed in rags of clothes, and rags of bandages bound both hands and one leg.

"I knew someone would come," she said in the same flat, ennervated voice. "I knew they'd send help. Look," she said louder, "I told you they'd send help."

Shadows moved around him, furtive shadows of the people they had once been, bent and shuffling, not quite believing in salvation from the infernal chaos, equally unable to turn their backs on the least chance of it.

The woman said to Harry – or to someone occupying the same

space – "I told them you'd come. I knew they couldn't leave us here to rot. Where will you take us?"

A voice that was also not Harry's, that was younger than Harry's and unsteady with horror, stumbled, "I – I cannot help you."

The woman stared at him, uncomprehending, fear and anger leaching in to supplant the vacuum in her eyes. "What do you mean? You must help us. You were sent to help."

"No. To – report."

The woman seized his arm in the talon grip of her ragged hand. "Report? What will you report? – that you found survivors begging to be taken out of this madness and that you refused them? I don't know who you are, child, or what you're doing here, or where you came from; but you're in better shape than any of us and you're going to help."

"There's nothing I can do for you. Let go of me. It wouldn't make any difference. Nothing will make any difference. You're dead now, only you don't know enough to lie down. Take your claws out of my arm. Stay back, all of you, keep away from me! Please, I don't want to shoot you. For God's sake, have the decency to lie still when you're killed!"

And then he was running, with the sound of his own shots and the enraged animal cries of people who had endured too much clamouring at his heels, with his breath sobbing in his throat and the shattered landscape snatching jealously at his undamaged body; and he kept running until he woke.

Lockwood had helped Paul to his feet and now he helped him stand. He was exhausted. Lockwood was again conscious of having witnessed something remarkable and not having understood it. He was glad it was over. He would be happier still when Paul got back to being his usual snide, bad-tempered self instead of hanging on his arm like a man broken by torturers.

Shah sat cross-legged on the ground, her arms across her knees, unmoving. Her face was buried in her sleeves and she would not look at anyone.

Harry Jess was back on top of his black horse. He had already given his orders and his army was preparing to move off. Of the three of them Harry seemed to have come through their shared experience with the fewest scars. There was a new depth of knowledge in his eyes and new shadows under them which together added a kind of maturity to his sharp, petulant face. Even the scar-tissue conspired somehow to reinforce an impression of new understanding. "Paul," he said softly, for the third time. "Look at me."

With an effort Paul raised his head, marshalling scant resources so that he leaned against Lockwood instead of being held by him.

"These people I shall spare," said Harry, "because of the horror I know will be visited on the Northlands else. But you I shall spare because I cannot think of any more monstrous or more apt retribution than to have you live on with memories like those.

"In the months ahead, or it may take years, I shall come to believe that you deceived me, that somehow even in the recesses of your own mind you managed to lie – or that perhaps you mesmerised me and I was never inside your head at all. It doesn't matter that I know now that what I saw was real: my mind will construct an alternative reality in order to protect itself from your truth. She too" – he nodded at Shah, still camped with her back to him – "will sooner or later find some way of blotting out the pictures you fed her.

"But you never will. You'll have to live with what happened to that city, and your part in it, day and daily for as long as you draw breath. I can't imagine anything more appalling, or more suitable. You invoked this daemon, Paul. Carry it to your grave."

He wheeled the horse and rode quietly and without haste into the glare of the desert, his weary army in pursuit, back the way they had come.

# Chapter Three

The final phase of the journey seemed to Shah little more than a succession of goodbyes. Tearful goodbyes between her and Itzhak, and hardly less emotional ones between Paul and Calipha. The prince and the poet parted with respect and restrained affection. Paul and Miriam made their farewells warily, cool, each feeling slightly betrayed: there was no animosity because each recognised in the other a mirror image of his own ruthless expediency.

And again at Leshkas, the shaking of hands and of voices, the promises – sincerely made, never to be kept – of reunions and social calls, the laughter and the wine, the amazed recollections of a recent past that was already a foreign country.

Accepted as a royal cousin into the palace of Leshkas, Edmund expressed his thanks formally, in a manner befitting a king done service by a commoner. He had the sense not to indulge in a protracted tribute, and only for a moment when his gaze fell and dwelt on Paul's arm with its livid, puckered scar did his composure flicker. Paul received his citation in uncharacteristically gracious silence and managed a slight bow as Edmund left the chamber with his cousins Leshkas, young men of his own age though smoother, sleeker, as yet unblooded by life. Edmund was growing sleek and civilised too, with every day that passed. In the fortnight it had taken him to service the Leshkas power-plant Paul had seen the easy living and the good companionship round off the sharp edges etched in the king by the desert wind, fill in the hollows carved by the ice and soften the stem lines of face and body.

Shah had seen it too. "In six months," she murmured, "he'll have forgotten. Oh, not what happened, but how it happened, how it felt. When he tells people how closely he shaved death it will be with a kind of surprise, as if he'd forgotten he was there. The scale of it all – how many fought, how many died, how the Ice Desert stretches like a captive ribbon of infinity – will be compressed onto a table-top, for him to mark where Chad was with a salt-cellar and how we came to Oracle with a finger-trace of beer."

"And us?" Paul smiled faintly at the door an attendant had closed behind the king. "Will he remember us?"

"As demi-gods. Heroes. Exaggerated, both better and worse than we were. You bigger, me more beautiful, Itzhak wiser. All of us braver. Oh, and immortal: if he hears that any of us has perished, save in the most epic of circumstances, he will not believe it."

"Will he return to Chad?"

Shah thought about it for a moment. "I doubt it. By the time he can he'll have made a life here. There are princesses as well as princes of Leshkas: exiled kings are a godsend to remote royal families bored, and loopy, with incest."

Paul grinned; then the grin faded. "It was for nothing, then."

Shah nearly said, "You saved we five." She nearly said, "You rid the Ice Desert of the Barbarians." She thought about saying, "There wouldn't be much more left of Chad and its people by now if Harry had been left to his own devices." In the end, though, she just shrugged and said, "What if it was?"

"Right enough," he said, heading for the door. "The dead can bury the dead."

In the mews, while Paul packed his traps and made ready to travel, Lockwood came to say goodbye. He looked different. Good clothes hid the extent of his deformity. Good food, rest and a return to the kind of civilisation he knew had ironed out the extra kinks born of pushing mental and physical resources to their limits; his hair was oiled and his beard trimmed.

But he would not forget the rigours of the desert, or the griefs and terrors of the last days of Chad. They were in his eyes, and for the rest of his life there would be nights when he would wake sweating with the memory, and bottles he would share because his story, which was too clamorous to stay untold, was too fierce for sober lips and sober ears. He was a haunted man. His ghosts would not drive him to madness or despair, but they would ensure that a record survived of all that had happened in his vanished city, and all that had followed.

Now, the gut feelings having faded and the sense of perspective not yet having come, the events too old to be news and too new to be history, Paul could not be sure how much of what he had done had been forced on him, how much he had done for the best and how much from sourer motives. He trusted Lockwood to do as good a job as anyone of despatching the facts to posterity; with perhaps a footnote that the Ice Desert was in these days a domain of gods and devils, and in order to survive it and work it and ultimately tame it men had to carry both within them: the divine spark cupped in the clawed hand.

For himself, judging without posterity's vantage, before the dust had yet settled, Paul considered that his success, by which all the rest was justified, was not the rescue of the boy that he was being paid for, nor the discovery of the girl Shah whose mind had already repaid him more than gold, but the removal of the Barbarian from the Ice Desert equation. Given a secure footing in Chad, the Northlanders would have sacked every city on the plain within a generation so that the disparate culture which they comprised, which represented the world's hope of real progress more than either old men plotting in radiation-proof laboratories or cold women whose idea of evolution was endless replicas of themselves, would in dying have ushered in a new dark age. Paul believed he had forestalled that possibility for the currency of Harry Jess's reign; and after Harry it could be a long time before the Northlands acquired another overlord of such ambition and ability.

Lock wood said, "Where will you go?"

"Back where I came from, in the first instance. I've a fee to collect. After that —" Paul shrugged.

"Other cities? Other lands?"

"Other worlds, Lockwood. I'm done here. I can manage without an inertial navigator: I'm going to take my ship and run."

Lockwood shook his head slowly. He believed everything Paul

said but he still did not understand. "And will you come back?"

"Sure. Any time you've got a megalomaniac to stop and you don't care what it costs."

"Should I be able to find you?"

"I doubt it. *I* don't know how to find the places I'm going."

There was an interval of silence. "I don't know what to say to you," Lockwood confessed then. "I didn't anticipate this. It was unlikely enough that either of us should walk away from that war, inconceivable that we both should. More than once I expected to see you die; I never expected to watch you pack and leave like this. Damn it, man, I'd as soon bid my right arm farewell."

He winced and Paul laughed out loud. "Lockwood, you're wittering like an old woman. Give me your hand and let that be an end of it."

"By God," Lockwood said thickly, his great paws clasped around Paul's, "I've never given anything more gladly in my life."

"Go away before you start crying," said Paul, propelling him firmly towards the door.

When they were alone Shah said, "Will they give you your ship?"

Paul looked surprised. "Yes, I think so. We had an agreement. I've been working for that ship for six years: they wouldn't dare renege." He thought about it. "No, they would dare, if they stood to gain from it, but they don't. I've just about exhausted my usefulness to them: I think they'll be glad enough to see me gone. An ion-drive battle cruiser isn't that much of a price – not to them."

"Who are they, Paul?" As soon as she had said it Shah could have bitten her tongue. She had never asked before, deliberately. All she knew of his background was that his people were very clever, clever enough to give him telepathy, and cold enough to rip it back. She had not wanted to remind him of that. Now she had.

He eyed her appraisingly. "That's right, I never told you about my employers, did I? – I use the word in the sense that you might be described as employing a utensil.

"The place where they are has no name. Except among those of us who leave it needs none, and we speak of it to no one; and it has sat there, nameless, unsuspected by the world, for half of time. It is the repository of all knowledge. Cultures come and go, wars flare and die, plagues fester and retreat: the place squats on, unmoved, untouched, seeing everything and feeling nothing. It dates back to that time I told you about, when the world knew more than it does now; perhaps it is even older than that. Its people, if not actually immortal, lead lives so grotesquely prolonged by the sophistication of their medical science that they might as well be. With the capacity for almost infinite lifespan and everything that is known or ever was at their disposal, they have less need for contact with the world even than the women of Oracle. They are hardly of the world at all. They sit in their nameless place and watch, and from time to time if it amuses them they interfere. That's what I do for them. I am their agent; anyway, one of them.

"They were worried about Harry Jess, afraid of him becoming so powerful he could give them trouble. They sent me to shore up Chad, or failing that to get the royals to safety: with them out of the way a well-placed missile would end the Barbarian threat and Chad could always be rebuilt. I think, though, they were counting on the king surviving. After he was dead and Chad was gone and Harry Jess was still around, I think they took a fresh look at the whole thing. I believe – I can't know, you understand, except that I know them – that they decided Edmund would never be the bulwark they needed against the Northlands; they thought about the disruptive effect of an excess king hanging around the Ice Desert with time on his hands and they decided to give him to Harry after all. Harry didn't track us through the desert to Oracle. He was told. No one knew, except Oracle who had nothing to gain by betraying us and they who always know. It had to be them. Also, it's their style."

Shah was having immense difficulty taking in all he said. Her head was full of questions, but one seemed more important than the others. "You knew they were prepared to destroy Chad? Before you did it, you knew probably someone would?"

"Probably – yes."

"Why didn't you *say*?"

"What difference does it make?"

"Of course it makes a difference," she cried, exasperated. "You let us think you had razed a living city when in fact it was already doomed."

Paul could not see how it mattered. He shrugged and got on with his packing. Emir watched eagerly from his stall. After a fortnight of easy living the camel, like his owner, was itching for the desert again. This night or the next he would sleep under the stars. His head weaved restlessly.

At length Paul said, "Do you know what I'm going to do, after I've got my ship and before I leave this dismal planet?"

"Before you —?" Shah shook her head and gave up. "What?"

"I'm going to circle on top of those bloody old men in their bastard technopolis and drop bombs on them. Then I'm going to take out the spires at Oracle."

"You are not!"

"Watch me."

"Itzhak may still be at Oracle."

"Then he'd better keep his head down."

"Calipha and the calf are there."

"Not up the spires, they're not."

"Haven't you done enough damage?"

"I'm going to finish them, Shah. They made me what I am – literally, my mother was a test-tube and my father was a micro-pipette – now they can finally face up to the consequences of what they do. They've already destroyed the world once. They gave it the bomb, and themselves the means of surviving it. They sit in that other-world of a laboratory, invulnerable, playing chess with real people, always sure that whatever the outcome of their game no backlash can reach them. But I can. This world will evolve better without their interference."

"And they hurt you," Shah said softly.

"They use people like tools. Manipulation is their opium; they are obsessed with power. They stunt the development of a free world."

"And they hurt you."

"They're too bloody dangerous to leave lying around!"

"You've a pretty poor opinion of the world, haven't you, Paul?" said Shah. "Do you really think it needs you for its champion? I don't know anything about thse chess-players of yours, but I wonder if they're as influential as they, and you, suppose. Time has an interesting way of dealing with oppressors. They are absorbed. In imposing their will on their subject people they are slowly and subtly drawn into that people, changed and mutated and made a part of them. That's how the meek inherit the earth: by accepting and enduring and ultimately absorbing those who would conquer them.

"The place where I was born sits athwart the trading routes, a natural focus for travellers from the pack ice to the Pewter Sea, from the western forests to the great lakes. My town has seen more invaders than the Ice Desert has seen winters: wave after wave of them breaking over our walls and flooding our land. All of them triumph, all of them stay. But the worst of them have not endured for more than a generation. After that the invaders and the people are one, a common stock ready to meet the shock of the next horde. But don't you see, it's the land and the people of the land who win through, and though the invaders remain the names of the invaders are lost. The people tame the horde. The world will tame your chess-players if the need arises. You and your battle-cruiser won't be required. There are greater forces at work."

She finished to find Paul staring at her as if she had quietly levitated. She smiled sweetly at him, thinking You'd better get used to it, hotshot, your days of having the last word are numbered. She said kindly, "Tell me about your ship."

Paul blinked several times in fairly rapid succession. Then he told her. He said it was a war machine which fought not on the ground or on the sea or even in the air but above the air, in the space between the stars.

Shah's eyes twinkled merrily and she suppressed a giggle. "Listen, you, stop taking me for a mug!"

It was as if Pygmalion's marble lady had stirred, opened her eyes and started telling him how to chisel. Paul hardly knew how to react. He had no experience of the relationships between free equals and in recent years had got out of the way of having his judgements challenged. He felt his grip on the conversation slipping.

"Why should I lie? There's a whole universe out there. The stars are suns like our sun but further away, and many of them have planets supporting people not vastly dissimilar to us."

"Paul, you'd lie the hind legs off a donkey but this is your best yet. I claim no particular knowledge of the subject, but every child knows that the stars are mounted on a shell enclosing the world half a diameter out."

"Dear God," he groaned, "now she's an astronomer. All right, you've got all the answers, tell me what lies beyond this shell of stars."

She did not even think about it. "Nothing," she said firmly. "What lies beyond your universe?"

"Ah," he said, momentarily discomfited. "Well, nothing, in fact, because the universe is by definition everything there is."

Shah was unimpressed. "I don't see where that gets us. Whether we call it a shell or a universe, we seem to be describing the same thing."

"It's a question of scale. My universe is so vast it can only be explored, a fragment at a time, by supra-light ion-drive ships."

"My shell is plain for all to see, doesn't need exploring and so doesn't need a lot of complicated and expensive technology that I haven't got." She paused. "Why a war machine?"

"What?"

"Why a battle-cruiser? I can understand that if you believe in a great star desert out there you might want to explore it, but why the weaponry? If all those stars are suns and all those suns have planets and all those planets have people, you *can't* have fallen out with all of them – not even you, Paul."

He shrugged. "I'm a mercenary. It's what I was trained for, what I do best – maybe, what I do better than anyone else. Once I have access to the galaxies I can choose my own battles. Shah, out there whole wars are fought between single ships – massive ships, massively armed, representing the sum of their worlds' technical achievements. Out there wars don't involve land, cities or civilians, only soldiers.

It's a cleaner way."

"It's still war. Do you really want to make a life around it?"

Paul thought about it. The terrible grin spread slowly. "Yeah."

"You're immoral."

"I know," he agreed happily.

Up to the very moment of departure, almost, Shah was not sure he would let her go with him. Her strategy throughout the farewell phase had been to stand beside Paul and say goodbye to the people he said goodbye to; so that in the end, without anything much having been said between them, it was Paul and Shah and the camel who slipped out of Leshkas with the dawn, unheralded, hours before the appointed time, before the hired musicians had tuned their instruments or the throngs gathered to paint the streets with their festive finery. Shah, secretly, was rather sorry to forego the colour and pageantry of a civic send-off and would have liked to wave to Edmund and Lockwood a last time, but Paul hated ceremony and despised merry-making with a passion.

www.ingramcontent.com/pod-product-compliance
Ingram Content Group UK Ltd.
Pitfield, Milton Keynes, MK11 3LW, UK
UKHW040640280225
455688UK00002B/29